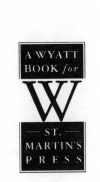

A WYATT BOOK *for*

W

ST.
MARTIN'S
PRESS

Regarding Roderer

Guillermo Martínez

TRANSLATED BY LAURA DAIL

A WYATT BOOK *for* ST. MARTIN'S PRESS
NEW YORK

To Eugenia

Production Editor: David Stanford Burr

Designer: Sara Stemen

LIBRARY OF CONGRESS CATALOGING-IN-PUBLICATION DATA

Martínez, Guillermo.
    [Acerca de Roderer. English & Spanish]
    Regarding Roderer / Guillermo Martínez ; translated by
    Laura C. Dail.
        p.   cm.
    ISBN 0-312-11374-9
    I. Dail, Laura C.   II. Title.
    PQ7798.23.A69165A3413   1994
    863—dc20   94-22225
                                                         CIP

First Edition: November 1994

10 9 8 7 6 5 4 3 2 1

Regarding Roderer

One

I saw Gustavo Roderer for the first time at the bar of the Olympus Club where the chess players of Puente Viejo gathered at night. The place was dubious enough for my mother to protest under her breath every time I headed that way, but not enough for my father to forbid it. The chess tables were in the back; there weren't more than five or six, with the squares carved into the wood. In the rest of the room, they played poker or dice in close, tense rounds. That was where the dry detonation of dice cubes and voices raised to order more gin came from, more and more threatening as the night went on.

Convinced that great chess players should remain proudly apart from all earthly matters, I looked upon that noisy world with calm disgust, though it did bother me—and ruined my smug moral superiority—that this rejection of mine coincided with my mother's virtuous arguments. I was even more disturbed to discover that the two worlds were not completely separate. I had watched many of those who had once been the town's most notable chess players now at those game tables up front, as if, sooner or later, some irresistable fascination, an obscure inversion of intelligence, lured the best ones over. I had seen Salinas, who, at seventeen years old, was the best chess player in the province, move to the other side little by little. I swore to myself then that that would never happen to me.

The night I met Roderer, my plan was to recreate a short game from *The Informer* and maybe play a couple of games with the oldest Nielsen brother. Roderer was standing against the bar talking to Jeremias. More accurately, the old man was talking to him as he inspected a few glasses under the light. Roderer, who had already stopped listening to him, was watching the swift spin of the dishwasher and the glass that shone briefly on the top. He watched with that absent expression that withdrew itself from everything in the middle of a conversation. The moment Jeremias spotted me, he waved me over.

"Looks like this kid's come to live here," he said. "He's looking for someone to play."

Roderer had partially emerged from his absorption; he looked me over with little curiosity. At this point in my life, I stuck my hand out without hesitation, because that greeting of men, dignified and distant, struck me as one of the best acquisitions of adolescence. This time, however, I restrained myself and just said my name. There was something about Roderer that discouraged even the slightest physical contact.

We sat down at the last table in back. In the draw for colors, I got White. Roderer very slowly set up his men.

I assumed he barely knew how to play and, since I'd just seen Nielsen come in, I opened with pawn to king four, hoping to liquidate the affair in a gambit. Roderer thought for a long, exasperating moment and moved his king's knight to king's bishop three. I felt an unpleasant sensation. For some time I had been studying that exact line, Alekhine's Defense, which I hoped to unveil in the Annual Open Tournament. I'd stumbled upon it almost accidentally in an Encyclopedia. Everything about that opening move immediately filled me with awe: that initial leap of the knight that at first glance might seem like an extravagant or childish move, that heroic, almost contemptuous way the Blacks, from the very beginning, sacrifice the most precious thing in an opening—possession of the center—in exchange for a remote and nebulous advantage in position. Above all, and this is what had made me decide to study the move in depth, I was awed by the fact that it is the only opening that the Whites cannot deny or divert to other plans. Of course, no one knew it in Puente Viejo, where they played the Ruy Lopez or the Orthodox Defense, or, at best, one of the Sicilians. I had been zealously saving it for the tournament. And suddenly, in front of everyone, this newcomer was playing it against me. Of course, it was still possible—and I preferred to believe—that the move of his knight was nothing but the clumsy luck of a novice. I advanced my king's pawn and, again, Roderer thought too long before moving his knight to queen four.

This happened again in the subsequent games: I precisely carried out the Encyclopedia's version and Roderer lingered over every response, always choosing the right answer in the end. I couldn't figure out if he recognized the opening or simply had a kind of lucky intuition that would crumble at the first serious attack.

Little by little, we were breaking loose. We were penetrating that no-man's-land beyond opening moves where the game really begins. I hardly heard the noise now, as though at some point it had been silenced. The smoky card tables seemed fantastically remote. Even those who'd come up to watch the match, those faces so familiar to me, seemed vague and distant, like swimming from the beach out to sea.

I turned to look at Roderer. I know now that later there would be women in the town who yearned for him; I know my sister loved him desperately. His hair was chestnut brown, with a tuft that often fell across his forehead. I realized he couldn't have been older than I, but his features seemed finished, as if at the end of his infancy they'd acquired their definitive form, a form that didn't match up to any fixed age. There was a brilliance to his dark eyes that at first might have gone unnoticed. A far-off light—I realized later—was always there, as if he kept it lit in patient vigil. When someone or something called them from outside, they brightened abruptly and looked with deep penetration, almost threateningly. But Roderer would divert them instantly, as though he knew his stare were vexing.

His hands were most noteworthy. But not even during the match, when I watched them move piece after piece on the board, nor later, during the different occasions on which we spoke, was I able to determine what was so peculiar about them. Much later, in one of the few books left in Roderer's library, I read Lou Andreas-Salomé's paragraph about Nietzsche's hands, and I realized then that Roderer's hands must have simply been beautiful.

I remember few details of the match now, although I do recall my bewilderment and my feeling of impotence upon realizing that Roderer was neutralizing my attacks one after another, even the ones I thought most shrewd. He had a strange way of playing. He barely registered my moves, as if he knew nothing about my maneuvers. His moves seemed incoherent and erratic. He would occupy some distant square or move an insignificant man, and I could reach a certain point in my plan, but would soon realize that, meanwhile, by one of those erratic moves, Roderer's position was now slightly different. An almost imperceptible change had occurred, but enough to throw off my calculations. Wasn't my entire subsequent relationship with him like that? A duel in which I was the only contestant and only managed to miss my mark. It was most curious that Roderer did not seem prepared with any kind of counterattack. No visible threat weighed upon my men though I never stopped feeling, with each one of his incongruent moves, a sense of danger, the foreboding that his men were forming something whose meaning escaped me, something subtle and inexorable.

After some time, the game had locked. All the pieces were still on the table. At one point, I'd noticed Salinas standing by the table with his drink in hand. As he drank, he broke into a sardonic smile that lingered even when they called him for his turn at the dice. Later I saw Nielsen leave; he waved at me from the door with a gesture I didn't understand. The room was gradually being deserted. Jeremias was turning the chairs upside down on the empty tables. Now I was the one who thought long before each new move. I had aligned my men against one of the pawns, a lateral pawn. This final attack, like all the previous ones, was revealed to be useless. His pawn, which I had believed to be weak and isolated, seemed better protected in each rejoinder, until it became inaccessible. I drew and gathered my most distant pieces however I could and in slow evolutions, not because I was even slightly still hopeful, but because I was too exhausted to try anything new. Once I'd managed to gather them all, Roderer unexpectedly advanced his pawn a square and his queen was face-to-face with mine. I felt a cold start. That was it. What I had so dreaded was about to happen. I studied the new position: The exchange of queens that Roderer was proposing would lead, because of the chain I myself had provoked, to the liquidation of all the remaining pieces. But I couldn't envision how the board would look. I could imagine five or six moves ahead, but I couldn't get beyond that. Nor was there any place for me to withdraw my queen. The exchange was forced. At least I no longer had to think. The pieces were falling one after another. They made a dry sound as they knocked against each other on the side of the board.

How many moves, I asked myself incredulously, had he been able to anticipate? In the end, on the sparsely populated board, I realized what this was about. The pawn that I had zealously attacked was free and advanced another square. I looked in search of my own pawns. I desperately counted the turns. It was useless: Roderer queened, I did not.

I gave up. As I stood, I looked into the face of my rival. I thought I would find one of those expressions I could never suppress when I won, a glow of satisfaction, a poorly concealed smile. But Roderer was serious and seemed detached from the game. He had buttoned his dark blue overcoat, and he shot an anxious glance at the doorway. His expression was irresolute but also irritated, as if he were waging an internal debate over some miniscule problem, some stupid question he couldn't manage to resolve.

Only the two of us were left in the room. What he couldn't figure out, I realized, was whether he should wait for me so we could walk out together or whether he could say good-bye immediately and leave alone. I knew this torment well. Until then I had believed I was the only one who suffered from it: the impossibility of choosing between two trivial and absolutely immaterial options, the horrible vacilation of the mind that oscillates from one to the other, discerning nothing, which argues in the void finding no definitive, guiding reason, while common sense mocks and incites it: *It doesn't matter, it doesn't matter.* How disconcerting to find in someone else, and in a much more intense dose, the symptoms of that ridiculous problem that until then I had considered my exclusive possession.

"I'm coming," I said to save him. He seemed grateful. I returned the box of chess pieces to Jeremias and caught up with Roderer on the stairs. As we left, I asked him where he lived. He said it was one of the houses behind the dunes, and that we could walk a block together.

Vacation was over and the air had that foreboding, heartbreaking chill of the first days of Autumn. The summer vacationers had gone home. The town was once again empty and silent. Roderer listened to the distant murmur of the ocean. He didn't seem inclined to start talking again. A couple of dogs suddenly barked on the side of the road. I felt Roderer tense up at my side, trying to locate them in the darkness.

"There are a lot of stray dogs around here," I said. "People abandon them after the season."

Roderer had no comment. I asked him which high school he was thinking about attending.

"I don't know," he answered in a serious, bitter tone, as if it were an issue that had already caused him too many problems and he wanted to put it out of his mind.

"Either way, there's not much to choose from. There's Mariano Moreno, where I go, or Don Bosco," I said.

Roderer shook his head. "I don't know if I'm going to school."

Two

As I recall, Roderer went to Mariano Moreno for under three months. He was already gone by the time they turned in our first report cards, and he's not in the annual class picture taken in July. From the moment he walked into the classroom, you could tell that a battle had raged in his house and that he had been defeated. It was the way his blazer seemed to annoy him, the sloppy knot of his tie, and his surly, withdrawn expression when he took his seat, not looking at anyone, not wanting to see anything. It was absolutely everything. Or maybe he hadn't lost the battle—and after meeting his mother, this seemed more likely—perhaps he had triumphed in the arguments, a transitory victory women often concede, but then later, with pleas and tears, she had wrested a promise from him. Now, he was arduously trying to honor it.

I was not alarmed, but actually relieved by his arrival. It's true that I was considered the best student in the class, but not even then was I foolish enough to think that was any big deal. Since my classmates made me pay quite dearly for my grades, I would have eagerly ceded my position. I realized quickly that Roderer had no interest in competing for it. From his second day, he paid no attention to the teachers and devoted himself only to reading. Oblivious to everything else, his was an absorbed, obsessed reading, as if the hours of class the day before had been a serious interruption that he could not allow again. He carried his books in a huge leather briefcase with accordion pleats on the sides. His desk was next to mine, and I could watch him take them out as the morning advanced, not worrying about their piling up on the desk. The books were always different, books of the most eclectic disciplines, as if Roderer were hurling himself into everything at once: philosophy, art, science, history.

He almost never started at the beginning. He leafed through the books going forward or from the back and when he ran into a paragraph that interested him, he could remain absorbed there indefinitely. Then he would remember something else and rummage through his briefcase to get out a new book. Having just read *La Nausée,* I wondered at first if Roderer wasn't like that ridiculous character, the Autodidact, who was determined to cover the entire Bouville Library in alphabetical order. But the familiarity with which he moved from one book to another and the strange preciseness of his search, could mean only that he had already read them all, maybe more than once, and he was now going back to them in search of something concrete, something which to me, in the muddle of titles, was impossible to figure out. I saw, underlined and riddled with annotations, the two volumes of Hegel's *Science of Logic,* which I once had vainly started to read. I saw the *Divine Comedy* in Italian, with terrible, somber drawings. I saw books that I would only come to know much later and others that were like painful flashes, books, I could tell, I would never come to know.

Every once in a while Roderer pulled out a novel that he saved to read on the patio during recess. Shall I say how humiliating it was for me—who, in addition to being a chess player, also intended to be a writer and believed I'd read more than anyone else my age—to see on that desk books from which I'd back down, books I had bitterly put off for some future time, or even titles and authors I'd never heard of?

But there was a deeper humiliation. I'd made a pact with my sister where, in exchange for some specific information about one of her friends, I had to tell her everything pertaining to the "new kid" as we left school on the way to the beach to go smoke together. Of course, there was never that much to say, but Cristina's curiosity was tireless and when she lost hope of coaxing anything else out of me, she made me repeat the title of every book Roderer had brought to school and then asked me what each was about. I improvised rough theories and worked miracles of the imagination to get out of each predicament, but at times there was nothing I could do but confess my ignorance. This seemed to give her incomparable delight. She would look at me incredulously and open her eyes in astonishment. Unable to contain herself, dying of laughter, she'd exclaim: He's smarter than you are!

*

The teachers were slower to respond than I expected.
Perhaps—it occurs to me now—Roderer's mother had
spoken with them so they would be patient in the beginning. Only Dr. Rago, as he paced up and down the
aisles, would stop in front of his desk. Rago taught our
anatomy class. He was famous for being the most
learned person in Puente Viejo and at one time he was
considered an almost miraculous doctor, but he'd been
barred from the practice of medicine after an unfortu-
nate incident. Accused of operating under the influence
of drugs, he had been scraping by ever since, teaching at
the high school. His disposition had become increasingly
gloomy. He was like a man already departed from this
world, a man who'd sworn off everything and kept only
a bitter portion of his intelligence alive. His impunity
with words, the insolent calmness with which he could
move from some scientific term to a scatological or out-
right obscene word terrified me more than his sarcasm.
When he entered the classroom all he had to do was utter
the title of the lecture to cause a tense and fearful silence.

"Teratoma. From the Greek *teratos*, meaning monstrous. A fairly unjust name, they are tumors of embry-
onic cells, they cannot be more monstrous than we
ourselves are. Characteristically, they prefer warm,
humid places"—he then raised his arm—"an armpit for
example. Like all good tumors, they grow over time.
And when they hit a bone, they start to gnaw at it. Understand this well: It is a slow erosion, lasting entire
months. They are infinitesimal perforations, absolutely
inaudible microfractures. And yet, at night, patients
often hear a characteristic chewing sound. *Crunch*,

crunch. 'Something is eating at my bones,' they say in the morning, and at first, of course, no one believes them. When the patients get to the hospital and the tumors are removed, they can weigh up to one kilo. They are the size of a grapefruit, with a capillary formation, an ocellus, or both, teeth. Do you understand?"

He looked impassively around the desks.

"Eyes, hair, teeth: a half-born fetus, under the armpit."

As he lectured, he paced through the rows of desks with his hands behind his back and always stopped in front of Roderer's desk, as if that were the moment for his own amusement.

"And what is our Louis Lambert doing today? Well, how nice: *The Magic Flowers,* by my illustrious forefather. The intrepid boy is now delving into the joys of horticulture."

But one day, Rago had a strange gush of emotion; he had picked up an ancient-looking book that Roderer almost always kept on his desk, a book with faded writing on the cover. Rago opened it with the half-surprised, half-amazed expression of someone who has found something he thought lost forever.

"Well, well, Goethe's *Faust* in the Rhineland edition," and although his voice recovered its ironic ring, it sounded curiously muffled. "So we know German, too. . . . This is good. It is fitting to listen to the Devil in his native tongue." He turned the pages and pronounced aloud:

> *Grau, teurer Freund, ist alle Theorie*
> *Und grün des Lebens goldner Baum.*

He slowly dropped the book back down on the desk.

"It's just that the tree of life wasn't green, at least not the sparkling green, the festive green of chlorophyll, but, rather," he said bitterly, "the green of moss climbing up a tree trunk, the fungous green of putrefaction."

Even so, Dr. Rago never spoke a single word directly to Roderer. He spoke to the whole class, or mumbled to himself without looking at him. The first person who really tried to speak with him was our literature teacher. Marisa Brun (she insisted with warm, stern emphasis that we call her simply Marisa) had studied humanities not in the Puente Viejo Institute but in the Universidad del Sur. She had blue eyes, intense, quick, slightly mocking eyes, the most disturbing eyes I had ever seen. She displayed her legs beneath her desk with carefree and happy generosity. Easily, she had easily made us fall in love with her. In one of her first changes, she replaced the old required high school reading with Tennessee Williams's *Summer and Smoke,* and she made us recite the dialogues of Alma and John in random pairs. The girl I got was so embarrassed she couldn't go on with the speech. Not looking at the book, Marisa Brun came out from behind her desk and nailed me with her irresistable eyes.

"Why don't you say something? Has the cat got your tongue?" Marisa said, taking over for my partner.

Blushing, I repeated John's words:

"Miss Alma, what can I say?"

"You've gone back to calling me Miss Alma again?"

"We've never really got past that point with each other."

I didn't dare look at her as I felt her hand brushing across my face that was tortured by acne. I didn't dare look at her as I heard the whisper of her voice.

"Oh, yes. We were so close we were almost breathing together!"

She was a wonderful woman. It was predictable, after all, that she would be the first to talk to Roderer, because even the most generous seducers have this prideful egotism: they cannot let anyone remain outside their embrace.

"Roderer," she said one day, interrupting a lecture, and she said it again, in the silence of the classroom, a soft call: "Gustavo Roderer."

Startled, Roderer lifted his head. It must have been the first time he really had looked at this woman standing in front of him. She accentuated her smile a little more.

"Stand up. Don't be afraid," she said, and in spite of her carefree, lightly ironic tone, I noticed she hadn't treated him familiarly, as she did with the rest of us.

Roderer stood up. He wasn't especially tall, but standing he seemed to dominate her. Once again I was awed by how strange he looked in the classroom. She took a step closer.

"Mr. Roderer: Do you plan to ignore us so cruelly all year?" And she smiled so imploringly that anyone of us would have rushed to answer for him: No! No!

Roderer looked around the room bewildered. He seemed to be seeing his classmates for the first time, too.

"Or is it that we are all too provincial for you?"

"No, it's not that."

"Then what is it?"

There was another silence. Roderer struggled in anguish, halting in his speech.

"It's . . . , it's time," he finally said. "I don't have time," and as if he had stumbled upon the only possible articulation, he repeated himself, his voice firmer this time, "I don't have time."

"Oh, I see: It's not that you don't appreciate us. You simply don't have time for us."

Someone laughed and then we all laughed. Roderer watched the effect of his words with sorrowful amazement, but I think spite had taken Marisa Brun over, because, so that the laughter would overwhelm him, she still said: "Sit down, please: We won't waste any more of your time."

As we were walking out for recess, turning down one of the halls, I almost bumped into him. I felt I should talk to him. I teasingly reproached him for not coming back to the Olympus Club to give me my revenge on the chessboard.

"It's just that chess . . . ," he hesitated, shrugging his shoulders, "never interested me that much. It was just an experiment, a model. On a small scale, of course."

I didn't quite get that, but it sounded annoying, just like when he'd said: *I don't know if I'm going to school.* It should have occurred to him that chess might be important *to me*. His words weren't exactly affected or pedantic. In fact, they were almost modest when he admitted that the scale was small. But this is without doubt the curse of intelligence, that even when you try to be modest, it comes out offensive. On the other hand, I realized, without Roderer as an opponent, I could win the Annual Open Tournament. This restored my good mood. As we walked down the stairs toward the patio, I looked at the cover of the book that Roderer had under his arm. It was *The Figure in the Carpet*. I vaguely remembered having read it. I said so and got the feeling he was glad. He asked me what I thought. I futilely racked my brain. I barely remembered any of the beginning, the dialogue in which the famous writer dares the critic to find the central purpose of all his work, the figure formed by the collection of all his works. The other characters and the rest of the plot had escaped me entirely. I couldn't even remember if I'd liked it, but I decided to take a little revenge. I said in a condescending tone, that the idea was interesting to me, but James's incurably evasive style had spoiled it. Roderer didn't seem particularly hurt, just slightly surprised.

"You have to read it as a philosophical text," he said. "In its heart, it is like *The Path to Wisdom*: Absorb everything, reject everything and then forget everything."

We had come out to the patio. From one of the corners, I heard the murmur of muffled giggles. My sister moved away from her group of friends and approached us. I felt that undefinable pride I got whenever I saw her. She was truly pretty. She asked me something that, of course, she didn't expect me to answer.

"Well," she said, raising her big eyes toward Roderer, "aren't you going to introduce us?"

I said their names and Cristina offered Roderer her cheek for him to kiss it. She did it in a completely natural, charming way, and Roderer, captivated by that gesture, leaned forward to kiss her. Then something stopped him, as if annihilated by some frightening thought, and he just stood there frozen and backed away a little. There was a moment of terrible awkwardness. My sister smiled heroically.

"No one kisses anymore in the city?"

Dismayed, he looked at both of us.

"I'm sick," he said.

Three

It's true, as I said before, that Roderer paid no attention to what was said in the classroom, but there were two occasions when I was surprised to see a hint of interest in him. The first time was during one of our math classes taught by Durel, a graduate student working on his doctorate at the Universidad del Sur. Durel only came to Puente Viejo once a week. He had to combine his hours, so his class seemed interminable. He had no facial hair whatsoever and a face so childlike he seemed younger than we did. To make matters worse, his voice was too low to address a class, nor was he capable of settling people down with a yell or a couple of loud knocks on the chalkboard. The inevitable came about shortly. From the desks in the back, Anibal Cufre and his gang started organizing the most obnoxious pranks. Poor Durel, who listened in fear to the noises in the back, finished his lecture for his loyal following in the front row—a few quiet, conscientious girls. I was somewhere in the middle. I didn't take notes for fear of Cufre's taunting but, on the other hand, a bit of compassion for Durel (although I didn't suspect at that time that I would follow in his steps) kept me from joining the general rumpus.

Durel had a fairly peculiar way of teaching. He always began in a mechanical tone, almost reluctantly, as if he profoundly disapproved that whatever he was talking about was included in the syllabus. Then suddenly, something, a formula, the name of a theorem, or a proof that demanded some detail beyond the trivial would seem to inspire him, and in enthusiastic rapture, he would cover the chalkboard with giant strokes and go further and further back in his chains of arguments, far beyond what we could follow. This didn't bother him; they were flights for himself, a refuge in the beauty of mathematics, as if he longed for the supremacy of that order made from symbols and inferences to settle over the chaos of the classroom.

It happened during one of his raptures when he was lecturing about the methods of mathematical proofs. He was teaching us Ruffini's Theorem and at some point he began a line of reasoning that would follow, he told us, the method of reduction to the absurd. "Absurd?" one of the faithful asked, who surely couldn't have heard Durel's last words over the noise in the back. That innocent question hit Durel like a joyful bolt of lightning, an unexpected path to transport him to one of his favorite places.

"Reduction to the absurd, yes," he repeated, fixing his stare on that poor girl. "One of the oldest methods of proof, a method known as early as ancient Greece, and that is systematically applied, without care, across the centuries, to the point where, if someone were to suddenly abolish every theorem proven by the absurd, the entire proud edifice of mathematics would crumble. And yet demonstration by the absurd rests upon the most precarious law of logic: the principle of the excluded middle, the belief that between being and not being, there can be no third possibility. Look," and he quickly scribbled an H followed by an arrow and then a T. "Look at the deceiving simplicity: You assume the theory to be false and under this assumption, you can prove the hypothesis is also false. There it is, the truth of T is confirmed. And why?"

Obviously, no one answered. Durel exclaimed incredulously: "Because assuming its falsehood has led to an absurdity," and he struck the H on the blackboard. "That the hypothesis is simultaneously true and false!"

He didn't find the effect of illumination he was looking for this time either, but I noticed Roderer had dropped his reading and was listening.

"In this way," Durel continued, "the most complex, absolutely fictitious entities can be engendered by a purely logical path, veritable monsters of abstraction that nevertheless have a virtual exsitence, sustained only by the trust of man and his way of thinking."

He stopped, breathless, as though he'd suddenly remembered where he was. No doubt he saw the blank faces, the pens pushed aside. Only Roderer listened to the end. He looked at his watch guiltily.

"Returning to the Remainder Theorem . . . ," Durel said, lacking the courage to go on, "It's not going to be on the exam."

As everyone got up, I saw Roderer writing something

in the margin of his book. As I passed, I looked over his shoulder and read: *To suppose that He exists, and not arrive at an absurdity.*

The second time was during Rago's lecture on alkaloids. This topic had been added to the syllabus for the first time and we all had wicked expectations about the class since the doctor's addiction was a well-known secret. At first, it didn't seem the lecture would be much different from the rest. Dr. Rago drew a rather artistic flower on the blackboard and wrote below it: *Papaver somniferum.*

"More familiarly known as Poppy or Opium Poppy."

He had uttered the word *opium* in a neutral tone, but that brief, ominous sound was enough to send a deep silence over the classroom. Dr. Rago explained the method of extraction of the essence and how the cakes are dried and prepared for commerce. He named the countries and regions where poppy was grown and spoke of the two opium wars; *1907,* he wrote on the board.

"Opium," he said, "was not always illegal."

He went on to recite an overwhelming list of its various medicinal uses and mentioned the derivative drugs in passing: morphine, "Our ace of spades in extremis," and heroin, which he pronounced contemptuously.

"Opium and the mental processes."

That title made Roderer lift his head. Rago explained in detail the chemical exchanges that set off the emanations in the hypothalamus and the subtle activation of endorphins in the limbic system. He, too, had noticed that Roderer was listening and Rago became even more meticulous than usual.

"Unlike alcohol, unlike crude, modern substitutes," he said, "opium does not simply cloud the conscience, but actually gives it its highest level of clarity. That is why it was always the scientists' and the artists' drug of choice. On opium, the mind acquires a new light, an immensely dilated brilliance like the original creation. It has justly been called the drug of paradise, not simply because it was the first drug that man encountered, but because it brings out the divine part of his nature, that part that man seems to fear much more than his demonic side. How else can one explain," he said as his voice rose irrepressibly, "the fact that legions of doctors and rulers have conspired to amass lies against it? And since they cannot conceal the miracles of liberation granted by the tiny seed, they set about fabricating frightening, imaginary consequences. It is true, as De Quincey says, that opium holds terrors for those who abuse its indulgence. And so what? Opium does not judge, and whoever looks for an inferno, it grants an inferno. Fear is too weak an argument: What will they say when, not long from now, they are able to line the hypothalamus, and opium becomes as dangerous as caffeine?

"Getting back to our lecture, it has been proven that in addition to that despicable English writer already mentioned, regular beneficiaries of the black pipe also included poor people like Samuel Coleridge, Jean Cocteau, Edgar Allan Poe (who, indeed, preferred it in its *laudanum negus* form), Théophile Gautier, Nerval, Michaux, Shadwell, Chaucer, André Malraux, and, it is said,

Homer himself. Let us say, to conclude, in the just words of O'Brien, that the opium smoker enjoys a marvelous expansion of thought, a prodigious intensification of his faculties of perception, a sensation of existing without limits which wouldn't be traded for a king's ransom and that I hope you, my good children, never ever try."

Roderer smiled and bowed his head. In that "good children" remark, in the gesture to include us all, Rago had managed to leave him out.

I suppose I should also include here a singular prophecy Rago unleashed in one of his other classes, though it pains me to do so. He was talking about the nervous system and investigations into human intelligence; he had already ridiculed those who toil at measuring Einstein's brain a hundred different ways and the intelligence quotient tests. He then declared that the diverse types of intelligence could be reduced to two principal kinds: the first, he said, is assimilative intelligence, intelligence that behaves like a sponge and instantly absorbs all that it is offered, intelligence that progresses confidently and finds the relations and analogies already established by others natural and evident, intelligence that is agreeably oriented toward the world and feels in its element in any domain of thought.

"Coincidentally," he then said, "we have a good example among us."

Anxiously, I noticed that he was looking toward my desk.

"Yes, yes: you, young man, don't pretend to be distracted. Isn't your name the one we see year after year on

Since Roderer's arrival, that curious human law, according to which the shyest person becomes the most desired,
had held true among the female sector of our class. The
bigger the barrier, the hotter the flame. One girl fell
hard. She fell with that undisguised passion, painful to
watch, the way charmless girls usually fall in love. Her
name was Daniela, but we'd been calling her Flowerpot
Rossi since first grade. She had extremely thick calves,
massive legs that seemed not to belong to her because
her body was quite skinny from the waist up. Her face
got round again and was sheltered by a chaste expression, forever on the verge of being startled by the first
crude word. She had a certain beauty, the kind of tender
beauty that is fairly useless and that, like a small consolation, tempers the features of fat girls. Unfortunately
for her, women weren't allowed to wear pants at school
and the required knee socks only further accentuated her
defect.

Her devotion to Roderer was overwhelming. Only he,

back then and about the cliché things we say about adolescence: the age of absolutes, the age of necessary cor-
ruption, the age of crying when everyone else is laughing
and laughing when they're crying. It seems almost like a
joke that these benevolent, reasonable, adult phrases
both forgive the old atrocities and absolve the old guilt
over time, but also unwittingly question it in every word.
I also sometimes think that we were spurred on and that
another louder laugh was rising behind our backs.

Roderer, of course, still didn't notice her. During one
conversation we had at school when we crossed her path
on the stair, I remember he asked me why that girl was
always climbing up and down the stairs, as if it were
some irritating mystery. I let out an involuntary guffaw.
Because she's in love with you, it occurred to me to say.
But I just shrugged: "She wants to lose weight," I said,
and he nodded without looking again.

The day Flowerpot fainted, it had rained and the stairs
had been covered with sawdust. She slipped and, clutching for the handrail, rolled two steps and landed spread-
eagle, facedown. A couple of students ran to look for Dr.
Rago who had just taught a class on the top floor. Rago
ordered us away, kneeled down, turned her over and
wiped the sawdust from her mouth and face.

"This girl hasn't eaten in days," he said and looked at
us threateningly. Two school monitors carried her semi-
conscious body home. "She just has to eat," we all said,
"she just has to eat a little then she'll recover." But she
missed the next day and missed the entire next week,
too. The name of the sickness started circulating in whis-

pers: "anorexia, anorexia nervosa." We were sorry when they told us they'd taken her to the hospital.

Flowerpot Rossi died in the beginning of June. It was announced one morning as we were getting out of school, and they took us directly to the wake held in one of the tiny houses in the projects on the Camino de Cintura. Her mother kissed every one of us. She seemed to know us all. We shuffled into a narrow gallery. Unable to avoid it as we filed in, we found ourselves surrounding the casket. I could hardly make myself glance at what remained of her: a bird's head, the dark eye sockets jutting out. A linen sheet piously covered her body and covered, more importantly, her legs. We looked at each other over the coffin, and in those terrified looks we said to each other, unable to believe it: *This was our fault.*

The mother stopped Roderer, the last to arrive, at the door.

"And you must be Gustavo," I heard her say. "Daniela spoke about you so much."

"About me?" Roderer said. He seemed to slowly understand what that meant. He took a step toward the casket, turned around, overwhelmed, and, as though he couldn't stand to stay there inside, he opened the door for himself and left.

We had one week until our first exams. Roderer did not come back to school.

Five

A little later, in the beginning of winter, I went to Roderer's house for the first time. By then, I had read the two Heinrich Holdein novels we had at home and every one I could find in the municipal library, but I couldn't find his magnum opus and literary testament, *The Visitation*. The town bookstore had disappointed me, too. Holdein, they told me, was out of style; the only two Spanish editions of the book were out of print. Then it occurred to me that Roderer might have it and I decided to go see him.

The house was one of the few left standing from the days when Puente Viejo had been the seaside resort where the governor summered. As dilapidated as it was, it had not lost its majestic air. It was hard to guess whether it was worth pennies or a fortune. In front was a tiny, exquisitely cared-for garden with a gravel trail that led to a porch tapestried with climbing plants. His mother opened the door. My sister had once pointed her out on the street. She was a short, pale woman, who had neglected her body over the years and now seemed to want nothing for herself. When I told her I had come to see her son, her face lit up. She was so ardently cordial when she asked me in that I got the uncomfortable feeling I was not only their first visitor in Puente Viejo, but their first ever.

She guided me down a deserted corridor. Our footsteps echoed desolately from the wooden strips of the floor. We walked through another unfurnished room and stopped in front of a door. Roderer's mother knocked gently. No one answered. She knocked again and told me apologetically: "He's always locked up in here, but sometimes he goes down to the beach."

Finally she decided to open the door. The room was empty. It was obviously a study, though there was a sofa with a blanket in one corner. The sliding window looking out on the dunes was half-open and one could hear the sound of the ocean very close by. The desk was not set against this window, but against the front wall, a blank wall. Several books were left upside down and many others were piled on top of each other, leaving hardly a free inch in front of the chair. His mother invited me in and that was when I saw the library. It occupied the long wall in the room and the full bookcases almost hit the ceiling. The collection was immense and yet I felt a beneficent sense of relief. There at last were Roderer's books all together and they fit into a single glance. Somewhere in the house a cuckoo clock sounded. His mother looked indecisively through the window.

"I think I'll go look for him," she said. "He can't be far."

"No, no," I hurried to say. "I'll go."

I opened the sliding window. Roderer's footprints were in the sand. They circled the dunes before heading down to the shore. I found him sitting under one of the tamarisks, his eyes transfixed on the ocean. I think he was startled to see me.

"Your mother told me I'd find you here."

I sat down beside him and I, too, stared at the ocean for a moment. It was the ocean of my whole life. I couldn't make it seem any different.

"You think better out here?" I asked.

"I don't know," he said. "I come to stop thinking."

He seemed to regret the dry tone of his voice. He looked at me seriously then nodded toward the window of his room.

"That . . . , sometimes, becomes intolerable. It expands and takes over everything, it wants everything for itself. That's fine: It *has* to be obsessive. But then, there's no way to stop it. I can't close the books and calmly say: We'll continue tomorrow. Coming here is all I have, the only thing that still . . . works."

He shut up, embarrassed from having spoken to me about that. That's when I asked about the book.

"The Visitation," he said. "How funny. Yes, I have it."

He got up without saying another word and we walked back in silence. He took long steps. I hurried to keep up. He didn't take the book from the library but from one of the piles on the desk. I thought he might still need it.

"No," he assured me. "Not anymore."

It was a single-volume edition I have never seen since. There was a trestle on the cover with a white cloth, over which, in sharp, geometric lines, like a cubist sketch, the devil's shadow was projected.

I was about to say good-bye when Roderer asked about school. I realized that nothing I could say would interest him at all. It was a clumsy attempt to be courteous, awkward and poorly timed, as if at the last minute he had remembered to be polite. That irritated me and I found myself revealing an idea that I'd only vaguely considered once. I hadn't even told my parents, but I was talking as if it were set. I told him that I was sick of school, too, and that I'd decided to work through vacation my last free year and leave town next year to study at the university. I was flabbergasted by the confident way I had explained a plan that minutes before had not existed. But Roderer didn't seem impressed. He asked indifferently as if I'd decided what career I'd pursue. I confessed I hadn't thought about it.

"Maybe philosophy," I said and searched his face to see if I'd hit the mark. "Isn't it supposed to be the highest science?"

Roderer pointed to the book I had tucked under my arm. "Lindström would say theology is the highest science. Though you needn't pay too much attention to him. In the next chapter he abandons the monastery and devotes himself exclusively to painting. Deep down Holdein believed, like all good writers, that the most profound path to knowledge is art.

"At the same time," he said skeptically, "in this era, what meaning can this discussion possibly have? Theology is dead and buried, and philosophy, the way it's been understood until now, is following its footsteps. At the university they would lead you in circles around the

Four

Since Roderer's arrival, that curious human law, according to which the shyest person becomes the most desired, had held true among the female sector of our class. The bigger the barrier, the hotter the flame. One girl fell hard. She fell with that undisguised passion, painful to watch, the way charmless girls usually fall in love. Her name was Daniela, but we'd been calling her Flowerpot Rossi since first grade. She had extremely thick calves, massive legs that seemed not to belong to her because her body was quite skinny from the waist up. Her face got round again and was sheltered by a chaste expression, forever on the verge of being startled by the first crude word. She had a certain beauty, the kind of tender beauty that is fairly useless and that, like a small consolation, tempers the features of fat girls. Unfortunately for her, women weren't allowed to wear pants at school and the required knee socks only further accentuated her defect.

Her devotion to Roderer was overwhelming. Only he,

who noticed nothing, didn't see it. The other girls laughed and felt a certain indignation that Flowerpot would have, as they say, aimed so high. They were the first to notice that she'd started wearing makeup to school and had gone on a diet. It had to have been a Spartan diet because her face slimmed noticeably. Her body, already thin, shrunk even more and looked brittle. She wasn't easy to look at. But her legs refused to concede anything and now looked even more disproportionate, like two grotesque appendages. Valiently, Flowerpot continued losing weight, but her legs held firm. This was, of course, very comical. The girls traded malicious looks, assuring her she was getting gorgeous, even though her face, from having slimmed down, had become insipid, and her enlarged eyes had a sickly sheen.

"Now, it's just your legs," they told her. "You have to exercise. Exercise!" And they convinced her that the best way to reduce her calves was to climb stairs. From then on, during every recess, Flowerpot diligently went up and down the marble double flight of stairs at the school entrance. She moved with her head bowed, her body stooped over, not stopping one instant, counting every stair under her breath. At the foot of the stairs, the boys marked the time of her step with a wicked chorus and she looked at us with fearful but slightly vacant eyes. Her lips moved faster so as not lose count. Just as she was about to reach the top, Cufre let out two long admiring whistles through the split of his teeth. Flowerpot responded by nervously, modestly tightening her skirt against her thighs. That made us cry laughing. I often found myself thinking, later, about the way we laughed museum, visiting the old embalmed systems. The sciences, it is true, remain—physics, or one of the natural sciences—but one has to be at least a little interested in the world, which is never anything but a mere example. Even so, one should be willing to be content with what's real, still less with what's provable.

"No," he went on, "I think that in any case, I'd choose mathematics, the only field where intelligence has managed to go far enough away to be alone with itself."

"And you never considered getting your degree?" I asked.

"Yes, I thought about it. As a training ground. It would have been an excellent way to discipline the strengths." He made a pained gesture, as if it were still difficult to discard the idea. "I'm going to study whatever I can, but not at the university. That would consume all my time and I can't run that risk. I've got to devote myself as soon as possible . . . to the other." His eyes drifted over to the desk and he sat there silently. But I was not going to let him think I was impressed either.

"The other?" I asked sarcastically. "What extraordinary studies those must be."

Roderer looked at me coldly. His voice sounded neutral, but something in his eyes was tense and biting. "Yes," he said. "That is exactly the word. They are extraordinary."

He seemed to retreat, as if he saw me as a potential enemy.

"Well," I said slightly regretfully, in as friendly a tone as I could, "I guess you'll tell me in time."

I thanked him again for the book and assured him I could make it to the door on my own. His mother must have heard my footsteps and met me in the hall. She nervously dried her hands on her apron.

"What, you're leaving so soon? My goodness, and I see Gustavo didn't even show you to the door." She shook her head in shame. I told her I had insisted on showing myself out and her son had been most amiable.

"Really? And will you come again?"

I laughed and answered yes and she looked at me so thankfully I felt uncomfortable again.

"I know I shouldn't intrude," she said, "but it can't be healthy for him to spend all day locked up without talking to anyone. That's why I wanted him to stay in school a little longer. He barely talks to me, and he doesn't have a single friend. And I thought it would be different in a town. I don't know. It scares me that he spends so much time thinking."

She looked at me in anguish, as though her son were now beyond her reach.

"Ma'am," I managed to say, "does Gustavo have some kind of disease?"

"No . . . , no," she answered, confusedly. "What did he tell you?"

"No, nothing really," I said cautiously. "But sometimes he talks as though he can't waste one minute, as if time were running out."

"Oh, that," she sighed. "He thinks he has a deadline; once when we were arguing he said so. I don't know what it means. Sick he's not," she said as though defending one last bastion. "I would at least know that."

She opened the door sadly.

"So you'll be back then?"

I raised my hand, smiling. "I promise," I said.

Six

As soon as I got home—and I think so as not to give myself the chance to regret it—I announced to my parents my intention to enroll in the university the next year. This implied, as they well knew, my leaving Puente Viejo for good. My mother, who vacilated between pride and sadness, tried feebly to disuade me and stay another year. The fact that I wasn't leaning toward studying the humanities must have surprised my father, who knew me better, but he didn't ask questions. That may have been, though I couldn't see it then, one of the first signs of that progressive disinterestedness with which, little by little, he was separating himself from everything.

Cristina, who then thought I would succeed at anything I took on, was much more interested in finding out everything about Roderer's house, about the exact place I'd found him on the beach and the most minute details of my visit. In the days that followed, I noticed that she stealthily disappeared in the afternoons. Once, I couldn't contain myself, and I teased her about the sandy trail she left on the way in. She blushed abruptly and looked at me with such pain that I instantly shut up. She became reserved and eluded me, as though she feared some warning or judgment. I'd never seen my sister like that, but I avoided confronting her or asking her anything. I preferred not to know, not to find out. Immersed in Holden's book, breathing the poisonous air that seemed to emanate from the pages, I looked up when she opened the door coming home from the beach and in her grave, transfigured face, I witnessed the ravages of love.

On an afternoon in August, one of the strangest days of my life, I went back to Roderer's house. The streets of the town were deserted and the icy wind chaffed my lips and deafened the ocean. Seeing me, Roderer's mother let out a cry of joy and signalled me to hurry and come in.

"My dear boy, you dared to brave even in this weather."

She led me into the kitchen, warmed by a large stove, and helped me off with my coat and scarf.

"Go knock on his door while I make you a good cup of coffee. Go, go; Gustavo will be so happy to see you."

I knocked two times, not sure that Roderer would agree with her. I found him sitting in front of the desk. His hair was tangled and his face contorted, as though he hadn't slept all night. Next to the couch a stove was burning. The flames projected reddish, restless figures on the wall, but didn't really manage to heat the room.

His mother came in with a tray and two cups. "I don't understand why it's always so cold in here," she muttered. She leaned over to turn up the flame and then poured the coffee. "I wanted to congratulate you," she

said unexpectedly. "Your mother told me you're thinking about going to the university next year."

"My mother, already talking!" I said, alarmed. "It's
not at all set. I have to take a lot of exams. I had no idea
you two knew each other," I added.

"I see her in the bakery sometimes." She turned her
head half-way toward her son, not quite facing him.
"How I wanted Gustavo to pursue a career, too. I told
him so many times." She touched my arm. "Perhaps you
can convince him."

I looked at Roderer. His eyes were burning impa-
tiently. For a moment I was afraid he was going to start
yelling at her, but when we were left alone, he brought it
up again as if it truly interested him.

"So," he asked me, "what did you choose?"

"I decided to follow your advice," I said. "Mathematics."

I think Roderer took my words literally.

"That's good, that's really good," he said pensively, as
if an important piece of a puzzle had found its right
place. Contrary to what I'd expected, the news really
seemed to make him happy.

Reaching his hand over the pile of books on the desk,
he said, "This keeps getting more complicated, it's getting too difficult not to require, at some point, mathematics. And now I will have someone to rely on: the
human element, after all. I can resort to the human element. That's it; you will be my eyes and ears," he said
enthusiastically, as if he'd reached a conclusion.

I looked at him. I wasn't sure whether or not he was
serious. It occurred to me for the first time that his self-

imposed incarceration might be driving him crazy. He'd gotten absorbed, his cup of coffee half-way to his mouth, as though he were tying up a loose end. Suddenly, with unexpected cordialness, he asked me what I'd thought of Holdein's book. I thought good-humoredly that if I answered well he might turn me into his allied serf. I started speaking, in the pedantic way I did back then, and I went on for quite some time. Roderer nodded attentively to every one of my opinions and my enthusiastic statements, but I realized he was waiting for me to mention something else, something more. His attention was centered on whether or not I would utter that one thing, whatever it was, and as he listened to me, he was growing disappointed. Slightly offended, I stopped. There was silence.

"Yes," he said, "that's all true." Perhaps to spur me on, he repeated one or two of my statements. When he said them, with no emphasis or passion, they sounded more or less like childish praise. I think he realized he was making things worse and he carefully started over.

"Everything you said . . . , I felt all of that too, exactly the same, in my first reading. They are, shall we say, the right answers, the finished product. But in a great work, the part that is incomplete, or unattained, the inconsistencies, the part of the material that couldn't be dominated, the points of extreme difficulty at which something has to be lost in order to proceed are also revealing. It's inevitable," he went on, "because every work, even the most complex, is a simplification and a reduction. To move from the chaotic infinity, riddled with only partially coherent facts and relationships, that is before him, to the finiteness of a book, the writer can keep only a few elements. He must arrange them in the best possible way to create the illusion, but only an illusion, the magnitudes of reality. That is the heart of the accomplishment: a rational simulation, an artifice. But in the mistakes, through the cracks, one can sometimes glimpse the true abyss, the original vision.

"Yeah?" I said, still annoyed, "and where is poor Holdein's mistake?" Roderer didn't notice my ironic tone.

"Weren't you struck, for example, by the theme of the passions? In the beginning, Lindström is described as a person with no feelings. *He barely noticed,* it says in the first pages, *whose company he was in: A frigid aura encircled him.* When he is asked if any passion exists for him stronger than love, he doesn't hesitate to answer: *Yes, the curiosity of the spirit.* Holdein was brave to write that, to formulate an entirely cerebral hero. But then, in his first encounter with the first real passion, doesn't Lindström cave in too quickly? Isn't the romance with the prostitute a little disappointing? You have to admit, at the very least, it's strange. Strange, of course, with respect to Lindström's personality. Adventure in itself is very vulgar, practically commonplace in literature, but you can see even Holden is uncomfortable relaying it. It's narrated, and not due to Puritanism, in the most indirect way possible, and since he can't justify it, he ends up referring to it as a 'chemical transformation' in Lindström's nature. The whole story seems continued. But why did he have to include it?"

"It's explained further on," I said. "It represents his undoing, the act by which Lindström sacrifices his salvation."

"Sure, that's what is said, but it still sounds like an a

posteriori justification, an attempt at artfulness to stop him from retreating from what's written, to save it by going further. It really succeeds only in making things worse. Because love can provoke a thousand falls, but not damnation. It's too sheltered a terrain for the divine; in every embrace, even the most seemingly depraved, there are religious vestiges, echoes of Communion."

I don't need to say how disconcerting, how unnatural, words like *love* and *embrace* sounded out of Roderer's mouth. And yet I couldn't help feeling impressed, because Roderer, who was my own age, seemed to possess profound knowledge on the subject he was addressing.

"Damnation," he said, and his voice waivered for an instant, "before recovering the eternal coldness, is, one supposes, a solitary act that takes place behind the backs of all men; an act, moreover, that must be so terrible to defy even the infinite compassion. In reality, there is only one unforgiveable offense to God: the attempt to take His place."

"Like murder, in Dostoyevski," I said.

"Or knowledge." And he must have noticed my expression of surprise because he added dryly, "not, of course, the four or five laws with which men amuse themselves, not the quota of tolerable wisdom, but true knowledge, the *Logos*, that the Devil and God safeguard together."

His eyes had hardened, as if he'd momentarily stopped talking figuratively. He seemed to see two enemies rebelling against him. He addressed me again with a tense smile.

"In any case, you now see that Lindström's romance

with that Mary Magdalene could not scandalize the Lord."

"It could be," I ventured, "that he included the story not because it was important in itself, but because he needed it later in the plot. It is precisely in that relationship," I remembered, "that he contracts syphillis and reaches the feverish point that later allows him to perceive the Devil."

"No," Roderer said, as though he'd already considered that possibility. "If it were a simple matter of getting him to perceive the Devil, there is another, more effective way than some venereal disease, much more in tune with Lindström's personality."

He stopped as if he weren't sure if he should go on.

"What?" I asked. I wanted to hear him say it. Imperturbable, he looked at me.

"What Magritte used and what Dr. Rago lectured so much about. It conforms perfectly to the era and would have been less artificial. Holdein has to kill two doctors to stop them from curing Lindström, two murders just to make the rate of progression of that syphillis believable."

It occurred to me that the reason could also be trivial.

"Couldn't it simply have been an adventure that Holdein himself experienced and couldn't resist writing? After all, in all his other books and right here, in a thousand places, he uses his autobiography: He is Lindström."

Roderer hesitated a moment. "It could be, but that doesn't explain why he succumbs to the other passions as well. His love for the Russian ballerina, for example, is not transposed from Holdein's life but from Picasso's. What I'm asking, don't forget, is why Lindström, the hero of solitude, who should be capable of turning away all feelings, ends up so vulnerable, or, in Holdein's formula: Why does isolation not withstand solitude?"

"Is this a question or do you have an explanation?"

"I have an idea," he said cautiously. "I think a writer's fear came to dominate Holdein. He was afraid that if he took Lindström's coldness to an extreme, he would become an 'unhuman' character, a symbol, an abstract figure. He formulated him, yes: the hero without a soul, the hero who cries out for a soul. Along the way, though, the literary tradition that allows any passion—love, hate, jealousy—anything but the intellectual passion, the old prejudice that identifies intelligence with frigidness—ended up squashing him. As if intelligence couldn't burn and couldn't inspire the noblest feats—life itself!"

Roderer grew quiet, ashamed of having spoken so emphatically. Just then I noticed he was trembling violently. I thought the window must have been left ajar and got up to close it. As I got up near the glass, I thought I saw a movement outside, a figure hiding behind a tree. It was dark, but I could make out a figure I knew too well running away between the trees. It was my sister. *Christ,* I thought, *she's spying on him.*

I turned around. Roderer hadn't noticed anything. His face, slightly illuminated by the fire was still and alert, as if he'd heard footsteps *inside* the room. I said I should go and he looked at me again, worried.

"But . . . we still haven't talked about the most important thing." His voice alarmed me: It was barely audible and sounded strangled. "The pact," he uttered with an anguished effort. For a moment I thought he wouldn't be able to go on. "There is also a contradiction in the pact."

He pulled himself together. He seemed to be once again on familiar territory, but the lucid tone of his voice contrasted with the guarded expression on his face. He spoke in a fast, tense whisper, as if he feared stopping again.

"What is Lindström offered in exchange for his soul? Time. Twenty-four years of time. But not just regular time, that is clearly underlined in the pact: It is a time of greatness, a time of exaltation, in which everything would move on high and in loftiness, the kind of time necessary for him to carry out his Herculean work. Right here lies the paradox. If it were just the old sand hourglass turned upside down, Lindström would be abandoned to his own forces. But, clearly, it couldn't be so, it cannot be so! Because the novel's great challenge is confronting the critical issue of art at that time: the progressive exhaustion of forms, the mortal inspection of reason, the ever-expanding canon of what can no longer be, the terminal transformation of art into criticism, or the deviation to other moribund paths: parody, recapitulation. And this problem, though only part of the other problem, only a question in the margin of the big question is so inherently difficult itself that it cannot be attained in any measure of human time. That is why the Devil must offer a superhuman time period, filled with nothing but fits of ecstasy and insight, a time ruled by primordial inspiration and an absolutely pure state of exaltation. Inspiration precludes choosing any alternative, neither improving nor reforming, *and in which all is received like a blessed sermon.*

"Now then, isn't this excessive? Doesn't the offer end up invalidating the pact? Because, in the end, who will the work belong to? When Lindström manages to finish his masterpiece, that 'sand hour glass'—which is described, not coincidentally, like one of Dalí's melting clocks—what does he do? *He destroys the painting.* And in his final discourse, he states explicitly that homage should be paid to the Devil, because all his work *is* the Devil's work. He says it in passing, obviously because Holdein was aware of this pitfall in conceiving his character. He knew that the pact presented as such contained this flaw, that Lindström could end up reduced to a mere instrument of diabolical inspiration. That's why he makes him remark that he must suffer and carry out daunting tasks, that the Devil limited himself to distancing the paralyzing doubts, the qualms of reason. With that alone, keeping reason in its place, isn't it all here, isn't it, in any case, too much?"

Roderer looked around and answered himself, as if unsure how long he could keep talking.

"It is too much, yes. Someone who was truly chosen should never have accepted such a deal." His voice rose. "And when the Devil introduced himself, when he appeared from the fire in his true colors and offered those twenty-four years? He should have said: 'No, I don't want them!' "

Horrified, Roderer went mute. His voice had broken

and that "No, I don't want them" came out high-pitched, commically flutelike, like the cry of a hysterical woman. Slowly, in all its inconceivable scope, I felt the magnitude of his revelation.

"And in that case . . . ," I asked, "how would the Devil have reacted?"

Roderer opened one of his desk drawers and took two pills out of a small bottle. With a gesture of exhaustion, he mechanically swallowed them, one after the other.

"How would he have reacted?" he said with no emotion. "He would have grabbed him around the neck and screamed: Then you will not have them."

"You will not have them. That means . . ."

"I think so," he said. He raised a hand to his eyes. "I think I'll try to sleep now. I can't sleep at night anymore: I have nightmares every night." He looked at me, and I saw that he was exhausted. "Have you ever had nightmares?"

Annihilated, I left the room. The kitchen was deserted. I put on my overcoat, not managing to button it, and I tied my scarf any way it would stay. Roderer's mother stopped me at the door.

"Son, do you like apple jelly?" And she handed me an enormous jar she'd made for me.

"Yes, very much. Thank you, thank you!" I answered so vehemently it made her laugh. And walking sideways against the wind, I held the jar tightly all the way home as if it were a talisman.

Seven

We were thrilled you won the scholarship. We knew they would give it to you, but, you know, there were so many other applicants. The fact that you are at the university at your age, plus the fact that you can now live on your own makes us twice as proud. And to think you used to complain that you weren't as smart as Señora Roderer's son. By the way, I ran into her a while ago, she sends her regards. It would seem she's resigned now to the fact that her son has become a ne'er-do-well. She told me that he hasn't left his room since he dropped out of school. He tells her that he is study-ing something very important. Can you imagine? And he refused to even finish high school. Of course, he doesn't consider working either. To me, it's a typical case of immaturity. He won't take on any responsibilities. What's worse is that they are running out of money. The poor woman is making macaroons to sell during the season. Can you be-lieve it? In the end, now you see, intelligence is part

of the issue, but intelligence with no will goes nowhere. What worries me is that, among so many
suitors, your sister only has eyes for that boy. She
thinks I don't realize, but a mother knows these
things. She even knows things she wishes she didn't.
And I know why I'm telling you this, even if it's not
a subject I should bring up here.

My mother also said in the letter that my father was
thinking about closing his studio. *He's tired,* was all she
said, and she signed off at the bottom with a few recipes.
So you don't eat hotdogs and hamburgers every day.

The allusion to Roderer threw me off: I didn't remember having gotten to the point where *I complained* that
he was smarter than I was. *Intelligence with no will goes
nowhere,* my mother had written. Deep down that was
what I had forced myself to believe, keeping it as an intimate trump card. But now, written by her, it sounded
like an insufferable, petty cliché, and I felt that old restlessness stirring in me that I'd almost forgotten since I'd
come to Buenos Aires. It is true that I could not have
pointed to a single reason for discontent. Life had
treated me with a great kindness that never ceased to
amaze me. I'd gotten one of the highest scores on the
entrance exams and during the second quarter I'd been
nominated for the University Olympiad. Math was turning out to be a game no more difficult than chess. I could
look at every one of my brilliant friends in school and
feel that, fundamentally, they were my equals. I realized
that they would not have escaped Rago's classification
either.

Yes, everything was working out better than I'd

planned, and yet I still hadn't managed to leave Roderer behind. The mere mention of his name by my mother had been enough for his shadow to rise again, and from its irritating stillness, begin to permeate everything as it had before. That bit about my sister, for example, was it just what I already knew or was there something else? Unable to avoid it, I remembered the scene I had had with Cristina the night I came back with the apple jelly from Roderer's house.

During dinner, we treated each other as if nothing had happened. I would have regretted embarrassing her again more than anything, so I concentrated on my plate and avoided talking to her. I was afraid that some inflection in my voice or a slip in the way I looked at her would reveal that I'd seen her. I was already lying in bed, trying to make sense of what Roderer had said, when Cristina came in without knocking. She was barefoot, in her nightgown, crying and desperate.

"Am I so ugly?" she said, her voice faltering. "So ugly?" And in an abrupt, desolate motion, she took off her nightgown and stood naked, next to my bed. Frightened, I got up on my elbows. My sister's shoulders shook from weeping, as she fell on her knees and buried her face in the sheets. I covered her with one of the blankets and for a very long time, I caressed her hair gently. When she could talk again, she told me between hiccups that the day before, she'd gone close enough to him on the beach to be practically in front of him.

"He didn't see me. His eyes were open and I stopped right in front of him, but he didn't see me." She lifted her head. She was astonished, as if the answer had been there all along. "He's on drugs, is that it?"

"I think so," I said.

"But . . . why?" she asked, imploring me. "What's wrong with him?"

I was on the verge of confiding in her the conversation I'd had with Roderer, but suddenly, even I couldn't believe it. It was as if it were a mistaken dream. I tried to console her.

"It might be just a little marijuana every once in a while."

Cristina smiled at me sadly and turned to put her nightgown back on.

"Poor brother," she said before leaving. "You never wanted anything to be too serious."

I thought that I was winning Cristina back that night. In reality, I was losing her forever. That was the last time she confided in me and from then on, she became impenetrable, as if she'd made some resolution that tore her from my side definitively. Of course, I didn't realize this at the time. I didn't realize I was losing her. I was playing the last rounds of the chess tournament and my preoccupation with the games kept me from seeing too much around me. I finally won and I had my trophy. When a picture appeared in the paper, I didn't manage to feel the triumph I'd expected. Roderer's disdainful sentence had done the trick. Roderer, always Roderer. And distance, I could now prove, had not managed to fix things. I tried to forget the letter, but in the months that followed, I started to feel a vague interference that grew to the point of visibility, like an image that had come into focus. I thought of Roderer in every one of my spare moments. When I left my studies to go to the movies, or when our after-dinner conversations were prolonged in the dining hall, I was overcome by the intolerably clear thought that, meanwhile, thirteen hundred kilometers away, Roderer was stooped over his desk. During all my downtime, he never stopped thinking.

I went back to Puente Viejo over summer vacation, after taking my December exams. My sister was waiting for me at the bus station. That year she had turned into an overwhelmingly beautiful girl. We looked at each other and laughed uncomfortably at the same time.

"You let your hair grow long," she said.

"And you . . . ," I began admiringly. "You . . ." But she hugged me before I could say anything. Outside, I saw my father's old Peugeot, perfectly parked.

"Hey," I said, "since when do you know how to drive? I thought I was going to teach you . . . , who taught you?"

She laughed again. "Don't worry," she said. "I taught myself."

It was dawn and the access road was deserted. I looked at the profile of her face, alert to the road signs. I looked at the beautiful angle of her neck, the mysterious and decisive change of her body, and every once in a while she turned her head and smiled sadly as if to say: *Yes, but it doesn't matter.*

In the afternoon, after lunch, I accidentally unleashed an argument at home. My father, who I'd found quieter than usual, had gone into the library to doze. Cristina had put on her bathing suit to go to the beach and when she reappeared in the kitchen, I joked out loud about boyfriends and suitors.

"Yes," my mother said. "They're lining up, but your sister is *Mademoiselle No*. Would you believe she preferred to go to the dance at the end of the year alone."

Cristina turned toward me. "Mom wanted me to go with Anibal."

"Anibal Cufre?" I said incredulously.

"He's changed a lot," my mother said. "Ever since he started working, he's a different boy. And all I said was that it made me sad: He'd been coming by every day with flowers."

"From Cufre Florists," my sister said. "The only person who would give him a job was his uncle."

"At least he's not a drug addict," my mother remarked nonchalantly.

My sister's face turned red with fury. "I'm leaving," she said to me. "I'll wait for you on the pier."

"Don't look at me like that," my mother said, clearing away the dishes. "I can't help it: I worry about my children. And this is not the capital. Especially for a woman; when she doesn't come home at night, sooner or later, somebody is going to find out."

I found Cristina sitting on the beach, clutching her knees. She had put a cover-up over her bathing suit and had stretched it over her legs in a feeble defense against the wind. The season hadn't started yet and all you could see, far in the distance, were two or three gray-haired men, probably my father's old fishing pals. I sat down beside her and took out two cigarettes. The wind wouldn't let up and it was hard to light them.

"I'm out of practice," I said. She smiled and stared a moment at the tiny ember on the tip.

"I smoked at home once," she said. "Not in front of Mom, but Dad was home."

"What did he say?"

"He walked right by and went to his chair; he didn't care. But lately I don't think he cares about anything. Some days he spends the whole afternoon just sitting. He's closing the studio, I guess. He wants to retire."

"Yeah, Mom told me a little. And how's she?"

"Mom? The same as always, and she'll never retire."

We were still talking cautiously, rehearsing the way we once did, as if unsure how much was the same and how much had changed. Mechanically, she grabbed handfuls of sand and avoided looking at me. Maybe I was staring too much. Within a moment, we were silent. We both sensed that the easy things to talk about were over. Then I asked her about Roderer. It was simply a question, but she looked at me furiously, and hurt, as though I had treacherously hit her.

"She sent you, right? Mom sent you."

I swore she hadn't, but Cristina didn't believe me. She buried her cigarette in the sand and got up abruptly.

"Deep down you're both the same, and you don't understand anything. You don't understand anything!"

She walked down to the edge of the water. And she stopped there, her arms crossed and her head hunched over. I watched the tiny figure trembling at the foot of the water.

It didn't take long before the same restlessness I'd felt in Buenos Aires invaded me again. The empty hours in the sun, the sleepy indolence of summer weighed on me guiltily. Even slipping my boat into the ocean, or going fishing with my father at night wasn't fun anymore. I wasn't surprised not to find Roderer on the beach. He must have hated the way Puente Viejo looked during the season, the sand littered with beer cans and the spectacle of people piled up under the sun. I had planned to pay him a visit—actually there was something I'd "seen and heard" I wanted to tell him—but some deep-seated resistance, perhaps stupid pride, made me procrastinate day after day. One afternoon, around the middle of January, I ran into his mother in the post office. I was waiting in line for stamps and I didn't hear her come up.

"Let me guess," she said and put on a comically fascinated face, "a letter to a girlfriend."

Laughing, I admitted it was something like that. We looked at each other affectionately.

"You let your hair grow long. And you're thinner. Doesn't your girlfriend know how to cook?"

"And you changed your hairstyle."

"You certainly are observant." She touched her hair lightly. "I had no choice. I've got a cyst here and it's grown a little lately. The doctors say it's nothing serious. But it's not easy on the eyes. At my age," she sighed, "you don't do anything out of simple vanity."

"How is Gustavo?" I asked.

"The same as always," she said dispiritedly. "Locked up. But listen, if you're still the gentleman I remember, you could help me home with this package and chat with him awhile. They're bottles of custard cream. Have you heard about my new job? I'm going to make you test my shortcakes."

As we walked, she chatted with that almost juvenile enthusiasm that made me feel vaguely guilty; I was only partially listening to her. I was thinking about what it would be like to go back into that house and to see Roderer again. Mechanically, I complimented a row of azaleas in the front garden.

"They told me they wouldn't grow here," she said proudly and stopped to contemplate them for a moment. "But now look at them." She leaned over to pick a weed, looked at them again and then smiled, a little embarrassed. "It must be because I talk to them."

She relieved me of the package on the steps of the porch and then went ahead to open the door.

"Gustavo!" I heard her call out. I went in and left the bottles in the kitchen. "Gustavo!" his mother yelled again. "A surprise."

Roderer peered through the door of his room and barely greeted me. He hadn't changed at all. Looking closely, it seemed that his eyes once might have been more brilliant and I noticed his hands had a slight nervous tremble I didn't remember. The room was untouched too, as though time hadn't passed inside it. I moved the pile of books off one of the chairs and determined not to take him seriously this time.

"Are you still shackled to this pile of dust-covered books?"

Roderer smiled in spite of himself. I went on, excitedly, imitating the grandiloquent tone of university performances: "Go out and see the wide world! In vain, do you wait for a dull reflection to explain the sacred symbols."

"The wide world . . . that's too old a trick," Roderer said. "That's how Christ was tempted on top of the mountain. All these things I will give you: kingdoms and the glory of the world. As long as he gave into life, to make him live a human life. That's his game: Extinguish us in the world. But the world is just an example; the kingdoms of this world are accidental kingdoms."

"Could be, but you have to admit some accidents are quite admirable."

Roderer followed my stare. Two girls coming back from the beach had stopped in front of his window. They were waiting for two others, who a little farther behind them, were carrying a small mat and an umbrella. As they passed, one of them pointed toward us and laughed. Before disappearing, the last two turned around and raised their hands to wave hello to us. I realized that at that moment I had a slight advantage: Roderer couldn't have known how much I'd changed that year. He didn't realize I'd grown up. This gave me a sudden feeling of impunity.

"That temptation," I said, "you are not going to be able to resist it."

"Of course I will," he said with annoyance, and then regretting his abruptness, he changed his tone. "If I know anything, it is that if I am going to have what has not been revealed to anyone until now, I must trade nothing less than my entire life. Don't doubt it. That is the price—my entire life—to find out the answer."

"But what if there isn't an answer? What if it could be demonstrated, for example, that the solution lies outside the limits of human reason?"

"If you are referring to the Kantian arguments . . ."

"No. I was thinking about the implications of mathematical logic proven not long ago, an absolutely irrefutable theorem. I heard Cavandore, an Argentinian mathematician who is studying at Cambridge and just gave a series of conferences in Buenos Aires, mention it. He said that the implications weren't completely clear, but it could be the last nail in the coffin for philosophy. What the theorem demonstrates, basically, is the inadequacy of every known system known. Every single system: from the most ancient cosmogonies and the great systems of the nineteenth century to the latest efforts of structuralism. This alone, though already impressive enough," I said, trying to repeat Cavandore's exact words, "would not be that new, because after all, the sensation of that failure is already present, in a thousand ways, and has been for more than a century, in the spirit of our times. It is present even in philosophy—from Kant on. The fact that the mathematicians are now putting it into formulas should not surprise anyone. But what is new, what makes the theorem truly extraordinary, is that the demonstration manages to abstract the very notion of the philosophical system and, therefore, it would seem that the central result could be applied not just retrospectively, as until now, to invalidate the known systems, but also into the future, which would annihilate the possibility of all future philosophical thought."

This last bit squarely hit the target. Roderer turned pale. Against his will, he said: "It sounds interesting; I'd like to see it."

"Yes, I thought it would interest you. I asked Cavandore for the references and studied it on my own. The math he uses is fairly elementary. I can teach it to you if you want," I said. For the first time, I was having fun. "Of course, doing the proof in detail will take time. There are a few definitions you should learn. We could start tomorrow or any other day."

"Today. I can ask my mother to make us something to eat later. Or do you need to go home and get some books?"

Roderer's imperious tone of voice made me smile this time. Earlier it would have infuriated me.

"No, I remember it well. I'll just need a pencil and paper."

I was, of course, talking about Seldom's great theorem, the theorem that was rocking the world of mathematics, the most profound achievement that logic had produced since Gödel's theorems in the thirties. It was already recognized that Seldom had gone much further than anyone else. It only remained to verify how much further. There's now a shortened version, thanks, I believe, to Lieger and Sachs. Seldom's original proof was long and exhaustive and I, naturally, had to begin from the very beginning. Roderer barely remembered his high school math.

He had given me a few sheets of graph paper with yellowing borders which I began to fill with the preliminary definitions and a few simple examples. We progressed at an inordinately slow rate: "one minute," he would say at practically every step, and he would ruminate over the simplest implication for a long time, or he'd ask me disconcerting questions, questions that would have made anyone else think Roderer didn't understand anything about anything. But I remembered a certain chess game all too well and I was not inclined to underestimate him. At first, I thought he was trying to test those mathematical concepts that were new to him within the established philosophical categories, and that he wanted, for lack of a better way to put it, to be sure he was understanding the terms of the formal language in their full range. But the distrust with which he analyzed every one of the arguments made me think later something much wilder, something incredible. Somehow it corresponded perfectly with his way of being. Roderer, with his half a class of math, was trying to detect an error in Seldom's proof.

Whatever it was, it took me almost a week to reach the critical results of the theorem. Roderer's mother opened the door for me with delight every afternoon and made us sandwiches for dinner, or brought us coffee when it got late. I was always the one who suggested we stop and continue the next day. When I got up from my chair, Roderer gathered and numbered the pages we'd written. As I left, I sometimes felt that the moment the door closed behind me, he sat down again and reviewed his notes all night.

The last day, I thought he had finally given up. He listened to me in a surly, almost inattentive silence. I tied one string of the demonstration to another, making him recognize the validity of each one, and at the same time drew from them Seldom's simple and miraculous argument. Roderer did not move; his face remained imperturbable, as though the revelation the theorem contained had still not struck him.

"We're not talking about philosophical systems here," I said. "But of course every philosophical system is an axiomatic theorem in Seldom's sense: the ancient cosmogonies, the Aristotelian system, Leibniz's monads, even Hegelian or Marxist dialectic. They are all concepts based on a finite quantity of postulates. The very idea of a philosophical system requires a determination, even if it's provisional, some preliminary notion over which the reasoning can tread. And as they fall within the theorem's hypothesis, they are condemned to Seldom's paradox: Either they are statable and in that case cannot purport great implications because they are too simple, or, if they have the requisite minimum of complexity, they themselves give rise to their own inaccessible formulas, their unanswerable questions. In the end," I said, recovering an old debt, "either the scale is very small, or they have insurmountable holes."

Silently, Roderer put together the last pages and the rest of our notes and then said good-bye to me coldly. When I left the house, going into the tepid, serene air of the afternoon, an unknown euphoria, an almost insane happiness, invaded me. It is difficult to explain. The sun had already set, but that vast clarity of summer afternoons persisted. I went down to the beach that was deserted, and ran along the strip of wet sand next to the shore. I ran like a lunatic, carried in the air by the deep roar of the ocean. In the weightlessness of my feet, I felt that life was once again enough in itself.

Eight

I did not return to Puente Viejo on my next vacation. I
wanted to "see the world" and as soon as classes ended,
I headed north with the money I'd saved during the year.
With no fixed itinerary, I crossed over into Bolivia from
Salta, and after two bus transfers, I went on to Puno in
Peru and from there, always by land, to El Cuzco. The
day after my arrival on an unforgettable afternoon in
January, I made the ascent to Machu Picchu by foot; rain
had been forecast that morning and the tourist contin-
gent had not come out. As I came upon the fortress, I
found myself absolutely alone, and feeling like I was
walking on forbidden soil, I looked out from the funer-
ary rock, on the sacred valley of the Incas. Shaken and
ecstatic, I felt my prideful atheism vacilate for the first
time, as if it would be levelled by that infinite silence.

Though I stayed in El Cuzco almost an entire month, I
never went back to the ruins. Perhaps it was because I
was afraid that a camera flash, the voice of the tour
guides, or an exclamation in English, could somehow
ruin that startling memory.

At the end of January, when I had decided to go back, I met an Arab archaeology student in a flea market. She convinced me to go with her as far as Chancay, north of Lima, to the kilns in the pre-Incan cemeteries. With the money I had saved for my ticket home, I bought a backpack and rubber sandals at a fair. For the first time I felt adventurous, irresponsible, happy. I let myself follow her from town to town until the end of the summer.

When I got home, I found two letters under the door. The first was a document from the army, with a writ of summons to complete my obligatory military service. The other was a letter from Roderer. I transcribe it just as I received it, without a date or heading.

I know I didn't thank you as I should have for the lesson last summer. All these months I've been over the pages you left me and as time goes by, my debt of gratitude only grows. It is true that I had a first moment of doubt, even hesitation, but when thought has gone far enough, all new opposition only seems like opposition: In reality, opposition points to the next height to be conquered and the reasoning seizes it in passing, feeds off it, and simultaneously suppresses and conserves it.

Seldom's theorem does not invalidate the possibility of a philosophical system. It can't for an absurdly simple reason: because I, as you guessed, have been developing one, a system that is certainly not trivial nor—I now know—is it inaccessible. And yet Seldom's proof is irreproachable and indeed reduces every preceding philosophical system to modest speculation. But it doesn't reach mine, which is of a distinct nature. The reason this is so, as happens in these cases, is hard to discover and easy to explain: It happens that all philosophical thought, until now, has been penetrated to its roots by a binary system of logic. It couldn't be any other way, because the formation of logical thought precedes all philosophy. Not just the methods of proof, the ways of validation or refutation; even the categories are hatched from the only logic man has known: the rigid, Aristotelian being or not being. And those that later tried to escape—Spinoza, Hegel, Łukasiewicz—managed to imagine, yes, what the laws and foundations of a different philosophy would be like, but they conceived it from the binary limitations incorporated into the matrix of thought. They imagined them like a man who only knew straight lines would imagine a circle. Seldom's theorem recognizes that essential impossibility, that original error. Another geometric comparison, perhaps more precise, occurs to me for you: if you think of binary logic as a true-false plane, Seldom's theorem encompasses every rational figure that can be drawn on that plane, but not one that would be sketched in space.

Not knowing any of this, I had begun from a forgotten page of Nietzsche about the formation of thought in the mind of man, the description of logic as the result of a long series of simplifications, necessary for survival, but fatally illogical: the predominant inclination to treat similar things as if they were the same, to underestimate the changing and the transitory, to omit the fluctuations, to concede triumph at every instance to animal instinct, which is faster and more active, over circumspection or doubt. He wrote of logic, in sum, as an old misunderstanding that the laziness of habit keeps us from seeing. The feeling of strangeness of my whole life was condensed in those few lines. For the first time I felt that maybe I wasn't the one who was mistaken and I devoted myself to rethinking everything I'd learned until then. I made myself begin with "preliminary principles," checking everything. You couldn't possibly imagine, no one could, the exasperating slowness with which I progressed, trying to disentangle, time and again, what habit had levelled and made the same, forcing myself to recover all the intermediary stages of thought, the precarious reasonings, the lost or forgotten links, the primary intuitions, and above all, the contents, that have been unbelievably ravaged, almost annihilated, by formal equalization. But over the years, I acquired a method, a faculty to discern, that transcends the human, a new understanding that will open the doors of another, still empty sky, that waits for men.

My triumph, however, is only a partial triumph. It is in jeopardy. I now know—you allowed me to know it—the extent to which I am alone. What remains ahead, the last challenge, is perhaps the most difficult: to make this new science intelligible to the old human reasoning. Can you even conceive of the wicked difficulty of this? Being healthy is not the same as knowing how to cure the sick. How can you make reason understand what it will never understand? How can I get it to comprehend me? Until then, I will be exposed. Wish me luck: I carry a flame of the most guarded fire, I head into a territory that has been banned from human thought forever.

I reread this letter many times. In the beginning, I wanted only to see in it the clear signs of some insanity, a kind of intellectual mysticism, or a sad and laughable megalomania. That part about another sky, didn't that in itself reveal a mental disorder? I also came to think that the whole thing could be a subterfuge invented by Roderer so as not to recognize his failure. Perhaps it was an ingenius way out: attributing to himself the possession of a secret that by its very nature cannot be divulged. The central argument and the geometric comparison struck me as convincing, almost in spite of myself. Why couldn't the rest be true? Whatever it was, I can see only the three words, *gigantic and pathetic,* almost hidden at the end, the only words that can justify Roderer's having carried out an action as strange to him as walking to the post office to send me a letter. *Wish me luck,* the closest thing to a cry for help he was capable of emitting.

In March, I began military service in the Seventh Infantry Regiment. I had not been fortunate enough to escape by way of the draft or the medical exam. After much thought, I had decided not to request university deferment. I imagined the whole thing would be a question of going through a period of instruction and that as soon as they gave me an assignment I'd figure out one way or another to regain the year. Reality brought something much worse. Before we had completed the first month of training, they woke us one morning at dawn, assembled us in the yard of the batallion's forces, and announced that Argentina was going to war. Galvanized by stupor, shaken by the officers' cries, we feverishly prepared the field equipment and before noon, we were on a military train headed south. The news of the war had left the country in suspense. In every town, at every station, the people were crowding together at the tracks with bass drums and flags; and in those enthusiastic faces and the incessant parade of hands that sent us off, I understood Roderer's sentence for the first time: *The world is an example.*

Very late in the night, we got to the junction of Urpila, seven kilometers from Puente Viejo. The people of the town had gathered with torches and lanterns and had lit a huge bonfire to wait for us. Desperately, I noticed that the train was not slowing down. I stuck my head and arms out the window and heard someone call my name in the darkness. I made out my parents, awkwardly running alongside the train, and farther behind, I saw my sister. She had stopped next to the fire, with her arms in the air. Someone was holding her around the waist, someone who was also waving at me: Anibal Cufre.

Our battalion was assigned to the defense of Mount Harriet, on the island of Soledad. The marks of time are curious. We were said to have been there only a month and a half. The night of the surrender, we were taken prisoner and, for almost a week, until the negotiations terminated, we were held in the church of Puerto Argentino. Later, they shipped us aboard the *Canberra* with the rest of the detachment. For the first time in seventy days, we could shower there on deck, but we had to put the same tattered clothes back on. We disembarked at the summit of Puerto Madryn, where a team of nurses waited for us with hot food and clean clothes. Shortly after that, I felt everything had ended. As I was uninjured, I returned by land in one of the army trucks. In the region of Puente Viejo, I requested permission to visit my family and was granted twenty-four hours with the obligation to report back to my unit the next day.

The truck dropped me off on the road at the edge of town. It was a cold, bright morning. The streets, the trees, the air, everything seemed untouched and glistened faintly under the first light of the sun. The door of my house was unlocked as always, and the smell of morning coffee lofted from the kitchen like a perfect miracle. Seeing me, my family exclaimed in surprise.

"It's me," I said, even though I wanted to yell: *I'm the same, I'm the same.*

They rushed to hug me, everyone laughing and talking at me at the same time. My mother released me to look at me and hugged me again. Cristina had grabbed me by the hand and didn't stop smiling at me between her tears. They brought another chair. I had to talk about the war, but I think they realized I didn't really want to talk. The four of us quickly fell silent.

"I'd rather you talk," I said.

"Around here, as you know, there's never too much news," my mother said. "But your sister has some news," and she smiled happily.

"Ah, yes," I said. "I saw something from the train, but I thought my eyes deceived me."

Cristina had gotten up to get more coffee. She looked at me, imploringly.

"He was mobilized in the second draft," my mother said, "but he was luckier: He was assigned on the continent. He should be coming back soon, too, and guess what Cristina promised him." She stopped; she was radiant. "Cristina, am I going to have to tell him?"

"We're getting married," my sister said. "At the end of the year."

I said I thought that was ludicrous, that Cristina was hardly eighteen years old and had barely finished high school. My mother smiled impassively.

"I got married at that age, too; she can wait to have children. What's happening here is an attack of jealousy is doing the talking. I'm going to find you some of your father's clothes so you can shower."

Then she called me from the bedroom.

"There's more news, not good. Mrs. Roderer is gravely ill, she has a brain tumor. You should go see her. She asked about you so much through all this. And she doesn't have much time left. She's at home now. They needed the bed at the hospital and they refused to keep her any longer."

I went to visit Roderer's mother before catching the train back. I had to ring the bell twice and knock on one of the windows before Roderer came out to let me in. He hadn't shaved and his clothes were wrinkled. He seemed more introverted and unsociable than ever. He looked at me strangely, as if my appearance were an inexplicable fact that would require a crucial modification in some hypothesis.

"I didn't think . . . ," and without finishing the sentence he clumsily stuck out his hand, as though trying to correct an involuntary expression that had momentarily appeared on his face, a fleeting but unmistakable expression of fear. How pitiful, and at the same time, how characteristic, that I would confuse things and in that single gesture of affection that Roderer made to me, I would think I saw a sham and would confuse his insecurity with an intellectual dread. In reality—but I can only reconstruct this now—upon opening the door, in that very brief instant of doubt, he must have understood the exact meaning of the fact that I had returned from the war unharmed and he did not want to listen and just stuck out his hand.

"I came to see your mother," I said. He nodded and led me through an unfamiliar corridor and stopped in front of a half-closed door.

"Are you sure you want to see her?" he asked. "She's had to have chemotherapy; she might not even recognize you. She's only sometimes lucid."

I went in. I saw the lumplike, motionless body on the bed. Her face was turned against the wall. The sheets left only the nape of her neck uncovered from which a few last withered tufts of hair hung. The tumor protruded taut and purple from behind her ear. I remembered the light way she used to touch her hair. *The doctors say it's nothing serious.* I took a step forward, not knowing what to say to her. The bed emitted a heavy odor of perfume. She must have realized someone was coming in. Without moving her body she twisted her neck and rotated her head toward me. She looked at me with just one of her eyes.

"You," she said, as if she'd been waiting for me a long time. "Tell me, you who have studied so much," and her voice broke terrifyingly. "Why do I have to die?"

Her gaze fixed on me for a second and then drifted vaguely toward the ceiling.

"You don't know," she sighed. "You don't know either." And turning her head, she wrapped herself up again and silently turned back against the wall.

I backed away, trying not to make any noise.

"I thought . . . she told me," I muttered to Roderer "that the tumor was benign."

"The tumor *is* benign," Roderer said with a cold rage. "That is his sense of humor. Absolutely benign. An osseous cyst. Had it grown only externally, the doctor said it would be a routine operation. They operate on them by the dozen, every day. With local anesthesia. But it went in through the brain. The doctor didn't expect it, but it sometimes happens: they reverse direction, and now there's nothing to be done. Just wait for it to keep growing and benignly divide the temporal bone." His voice went hoarse. "I thought it was enough that I stopped talking to her, that I had separated her enough." He smiled through a grimace. "I must be very close," he said and suddenly he looked at me again. "Get Cristina. Take her out of here immediately."

My sister's name on Roderer's tongue struck me deeply.

"Cristina," I said dryly, "is about to get married."

"Do you still not understand? Or do you think the wedding march is going to stop him? I know what you're thinking, I know exactly what you think, but you should at least remember this: Anything that provokes an effect, exists, it is also real."

And as he opened the door for me, he said again, "Take her away."

Nine

During the time I lived in Buenos Aires, my sister wrote me only three letters. In the first two—one for each birthday, she painfully betrayed a hard-won, sustained effort not to mention a name—beneath her breezy and funny commentaries. I received the last letter on a particularly decisive day for me. Cavandore was back in Buenos Aires. Almost three years had passed since the war. Argentina was about to reestablish diplomatic relations with the United Kingdom and in a show of good faith, the Royal Council had sent him to offer a scholarship program at Cambridge for graduating students. I was attending his seminar and that day, during one of the breaks, he called me aside.

"Why haven't you signed up for the program yet? You are one of the people I was thinking of. I have talked to your professors. They all recommend you."

Cavandore looked me over with serene, kind eyes. I felt embarrassed. I knew that whatever I said—especially the truth—would sound puerile.

"If it were just somewhere else, some other country. But England . . ."

"What do you mean? If you want to study logic, it is unsurpassable. Seldom himself will be there next term." He looked at me as though he'd just been struck by an idea too absurd to have occurred to him before. "Or are you making this an issue of patriotism?"

"No, it's not patriotism, but I . . . I was in the Falkland Islands," I said.

Cavandore was quiet for a moment.

"Forgive me, I didn't know." And he seemed to be reflecting on a problem that had become slightly more difficult. "I understand, don't think I don't understand. But look at it this way: The place is Cambridge, not England. A mathematician's country is the universities of the whole world. Promise me you'll think about it."

I promised him without conviction.

"I'm going to tell you something harsh, to assure myself that you will think hard about this: You believe that you are young, you believe you have a lot of time ahead of you, and all options from which to choose. But it's not true: you're not so young anymore and the doors that close now will not open again."

I walked back from campus the long way toward the river, and I continued along the slope to the docks. Every once in a while, the enormous, violent planes that took off from the airport deafened the air. By the time I crossed through the woods and got to the Plaza Italia, it was almost night. In the door of the building, the doorman handed me Cristina's letter. It started out in the same tone as the others, but on the second page she had scribbled a postscript under her name that seemed written in a rage and that ended in an unexpectedly practical way, as though she'd regretted the impulse half-way through it.

The wedding won't take place this year either. I don't know what's wrong with me. Or actually, I do know. I can't stop seeing him. But now I think he needs me, too. Ever since his mother died, the house is in shambles. He barely has enough to eat. Some days he has nothing but tea. A while ago, I was able to persuade him to sell some furniture, but that money is already spent. Later, he himself suggested we sell his books. I had thought about it, too, but I never would have dared to suggest it. Like in the Apocalypse, he said, the devouring of the book. And even if you won't believe it, he was in happy about it. He almost seemed content. It doesn't matter. I won't be needing them anymore, he said when we were packing them in the boxes. I've already been the camel in the desert and the lion, all I have left is the transformation into a child and children don't need so many books. Does that mean something? I know that he now goes to the Olympus Club every day; they tell me he gets there around seven in the evening, he orders coffee and stays there alone, sitting at a table, until they close. Anyway, I thought the epistemology collection or the Bertrand Russell books might interest you. Don't forget to tell me either way.

I took the letter into the kitchen and as I warmed my dinner I reread the postscript. Roderer had forsaken everything. What else could the decision to get rid of his books mean? And yet I couldn't believe that Cristina would be wrong about his mood or much less that he could feign a feeling. Then why was he so happy? Nor did the sentence about lions and camels shed any light. It must be true that for every desire there is a mortification or perhaps, simply, there are things that can't be seen before their time. These are small, maddening mysteries that lurk in the darkness for their perfect occasion. To know if Roderer had in fact given up was the only thing I cared about at that moment. It was the news I'd waited for all those years, but my sister's letter, with exemplary irony, stopped short of providing definitive confirmation.

That night I slept briefly and uneasily, but the next day I woke with my usual good spirits. I put the letter in a drawer without rereading it. Confident and resolved, I added my name to the foot of Cavandore's list. That simple act, like a warning that going to Cambridge would not be so easy, burdened me with the most intricate procedures and papers I have ever had to confront. There were barely two months before the beginning of the academic year at Cambridge and Cavandore insisted we be there the first day. I had written a short letter home announcing my decision and I had to swear to my mother on the phone that I would come to Puente Viejo to say good-bye. Over the years the time between my visits had grown, and during the last vacation, burying myself in my studies, I'd avoided going back. This, of course, had earned me endless reproaches, pleas, inquisitions, and finally a long, offended silence that this phone call of hers had broken for the first time.

I promised to spend ten days in Puente Viejo. It was then as if it were a perfect, storybook punishment. The dates started to run together unmanageable against my will and forced me to postpone the trip from week to week until I had only two days before my flight left. Of that chaotic period, of coming and going from offices, of the arbitrary, ridiculous bureaucracy, of the incredible hassles that entangled me at every step, I keenly remember the sharp feeling of strangeness when I finally closed and left on the bed, in the already empty apartment, the two suitcases I was going to take on the plane and packed my bag with the change of clothes I would need in Puente Viejo. It was like a sensation of the future anticipated in time: the sensation of not belonging anywhere.

Ten

The bus arrived in Puente Viejo around noon. It was one of the last days of October and FOR RENT signs already hung on some of the vacation houses along the access road. As the bus climbed the hill toward the station, I saw the town stretched out between the pine trees and felt that strange peacefulness again, that intimate disbelief that was my last resort argument whenever I thought about Roderer: Nothing excessive could happen in Puente Viejo. The ocean appeared gray and choppy. The wind blew a string of clouds that covered the sky and even that storm advancing over the town seemed a disproportionate threat.

Lunch at my house was lifeless. For the first time I saw my parents as old and tired. Much more striking was the effect that a new sadness, a fresh and declared pain—that was not, of course, due to my departure—had ravaged on Cristina's face. It was like something in her had given up and a well of bitterness had filtered subtley, irreparably into her features. While I couldn't imagine the reason for this new sorrow, I was sure, on the other hand, who was responsible for it.

We'd spoken at the table about my trip.

"At any rate," my mother had said at one point, "you'll be home within a year."

Then there was nothing I could do but tell them everything.

"There is something I didn't write in my letter. The program offers a scholarship extension for a doctorate."

My mother, who had started to serve dessert, looked at me uneasily.

"And how much time would that take?"

"Four more years."

I heard her muffle a wail and I lowered my head to my plate. My father spoke in his slow, asthmatic voice:

"You're not coming back."

"Of course not," Cristina said like an echo, "Like he's going to come back."

We silently finished eating. My father, not waiting for coffee, as if he couldn't break a habit, took the paper and went to the library. While Cristina cleared the table, my mother disappeared for a minute and came back with a large package.

"We bought you a present," she said.

I untied the ribbon and ripped open the wrapping: It was a bomber jacket.

"For when you saunter through London," Cristina said. "Come on, try it on."

Suddenly, an alarm clock went off in her room. My sister went to turn it off and my mother followed her into the room. I heard the muddled exchange of an argument.

"Not even today, the one day your brother comes home."

"You know I have to go every eight hours. I'll try to come back soon." My sister seemed to cover the entire room, gathering things. I heard the knock of a drawer, the sound of rattling jars, a purse snapping closed.

"How long? How long, I ask."

Then I heard Cristina's furious voice: "Don't worry, sooner than you think."

There was silence and in a different tone of voice as though slightly regretful, my mother said, "Do you at least remember that I invited Anibal to dinner?"

"I'll try to come back soon," Cristina repeated. She passed in front of me, lifted the collar of my bomber jacket and gave me a quick kiss. "The little English girls are going to die of love."

My mother left the room when she heard the door. I thought she would say something, but she seemed resigned, as though she understood we were both beyond her reach. Indifferently, she held out her hand.

"Take it off," she muttered. "I'm going to reinforce the buttons."

I went to the library. My father had fallen asleep with the paper over his chest. Soon I found myself wandering around the house alone. I opened the door to my room; everything was still there, like a trap: my bed, the desk, the posters on the wall, the trophy I'd won in the chess tournament. When I was about to go into the living room, I was able to make out beyond the bedroom door, my mother. She was sitting on the edge of the bed with her back turned and her sewing kit open on the night table. She was leaning over the bomber jacket strangely, with her forehead practically touching the material. It took me a minute to realize she was crying. She took off her steamed-up glasses, rubbed them with a handkerchief, and with a trembling hand, rethreaded the needle to finish her sewing.

Silently, I retraced my footsteps and sat down in the library next to my father. I saw the unopened fishing club magazines in their plastic envelopes piled up on the desk. I picked up the most recent one: On the cover was an advertisement for Twenty-four Hours in San Blas. My father wriggled in his chair and opened his eyes. He seemed a little embarrassed that I'd found him sleeping.

"Is it true you've given up fishing?"

"It's true, yes."

"That's what Mom said, but I couldn't believe it. Aren't you even going to San Blas?"

"No, I don't think so," he said. He closed his eyes again and leaned back to go back to sleep. "There comes a time when even the things you like best start to make you tired. You've got to get used to it. But it's fine this way. It's the mercy of old age: Life makes you tired."

My mother appeared in the doorway, her nose was red, the bomber jacket was carefully folded in her hands.

"I thought I'd make you an apple tart to go with your tea," she said, and asked me to go with her to the kitchen. She wanted to know what clothes I'd packed in my suitcases and where I was going to stay when I arrived. I realized she wasn't fully listening to me. As she stirred, she looked outside every once in a while, guarding the door. I knew she wouldn't tell me anything about Cristina. Maybe she decided it was too painful to deal with on that one day, or perhaps she felt I was already too far away, that I was about to turn into a stranger, someone with no reason to know her shameful secrets. And I decided not to ask either. This time it was not to avoid learning something bad about a person I adored, but because that was exactly how I felt: like a stranger who no longer had any rights to the family affairs.

Cristina came back as tea was served. Her face serious and absorbed, she sat down with us at the table. She didn't even try her tart. We could barely sustain a conversation. Time was held up with that heaviness of a small town that I wasn't used to. Finally, I heard the afternoon church bells, deep and solemn. When I got up, my mother looked at me with hurt surprise.

"You're leaving, too?"

"I want to go down to the ocean for a minute," I said. "Before it gets dark."

"Don't be long," she begged me. "I invited your sister's fiancé to dinner."

It was harsh outside. It hadn't rained but the clouds were compact and dense. The wind blew harder now and carried drops of the ocean water. I crossed the plaza diagonally toward the Olympus Club. On the short staircase that led to the game room, I was overcome by that feeling of deathly realism with which the places to which you thought you'd never return, come to life again and appear whole, exact, flawless. Little had changed.

Jeremias was behind the bar, and I could have recognized everyone at the tables. I ordered a beer and let Jeremias tell me about who had left town and who had died.

There was the same raging noise of dice and bottles, the same smoke. Now that spectacle seemed incredibly inoffensive. It was just tired older men on their way home from work and betting for their gin before going home. I noticed that now no one was playing chess. There was a single squared table left in the back. Somebody called out my nickname that I'd almost forgotten. I saw it was Nielsen. I waved from the distance and a few hands waved.

I finished my beer and was about to ask Jeremias about Roderer when I saw him appear on the steps. He had stopped on the last step. He stood immobile, with his left hand grasping the top of the banister, as if he couldn't get his breath. Only when he turned to come in, did I see the cane in his other hand. I got up to help him but he braced himself on the back of a chair, and pointed out a table in the back with a nod. The room suddenly went silent. All eyes followed his faltering path, as if they'd placed bets on whether or not he could make it alone. He had barely sat down when the noise picked up again. Exhausted, Roderer leaned back, and placed the cane over his knees.

"Now you see," he said, as if it weren't worth talking about. "It doesn't matter as long as I could get up and come."

Not very confidently, I searched his face for the traces of the sickness. At least I can say this is my defense, sitting there, his breathing steadied. He truly seemed nothing more than slightly feverish. I noted there was something remarkable about his features, an unnatural stiffness, a kind of absence of reality. It took me a moment to determine what it was. In all those years, his face had not changed at all. It didn't have one more line, not one sign, not one mark. Roderer had not been exposed to life. In mocking respect, life had passed him by, not touching him.

"Cristina told me you're about to leave."

I nodded. By an old reflex, I spoke of Cambridge with an enthusiasm that wasn't entirely authentic.

"Cambridge," Roderer said. "That's farther away every day."

I told him I'd be studying with Seldom, and Roderer made a distracted gesture of acknowledgment as if I had mentioned some remote memory. I kept talking in spite of everything, not because I thought it might interest or impress him, none of that. I was afraid to shut up and give him his turn. It is amazing what one ends up saying when set on not stopping. I was making a kind of balance sheet of my life—of what I thought was a life—in a complacent, almost defiant tone of voice. It was a ridiculous exhibition of my small triumphs and everything I added only managed to make the previous statements worse. It was probably the embarrassment of listening to myself that finally made me shut up.

Roderer leaned over the table. Only then did I notice how much he had been controlling his impatience. He looked behind him, as if afraid someone else might hear him and almost whispered to me:

"I finished it."

I saw a sparkle in his eyes that was not the shine of the fever or that old vigilant light, but pride, pure, old-fashioned, human pride. *A weakness,* I thought.

"You finished . . . what?" I asked calmly.

Roderer looked at me surprised, as if I couldn't possibly not remember.

"What I wrote you in that letter. What Spinoza and De Quincey attempted, the great vision that Nietzsche pursued: a new human understanding."

"I thought you had abandoned that . . . ," I said. I almost said "that madness," but his new hint of pride made me hesitate again. It was a weakness, yes, but it could also be a test.

"You thought I'd abandoned it? I don't understand." And he looked at me truly bewildered. As I spoke, I felt I was sliding into another defeat.

"Cristina said you sold your books."

"Oh, the books." And he smiled as if my interpretation were funny. "I just followed the road until it ended; I had already taken everything from them and then I destroyed them. Innocence and oblivion, he who lost his world wants to win his world. I came here and stopped thinking, I sat down to wait for the ultimate revelation to make its secret play, for it alone to close the great figure. It's true, it was slow. It may have been too slow. But now," he said, "all I have to do is write it."

"What?" I was shocked. "You mean you don't have anything written down?"

"No," Roderer said. "And I don't think I can write it. But don't worry, I knew you would come and I've been thinking about it a lot. I'm going to tell it to you and you're going to write it for me." He smiled as if he wanted to share an old joke. "Great, yet simple. Simple, yet great. I won't need more than two or three days, but we should start as soon as possible."

"But . . . didn't Cristina tell you? I'm leaving tomorrow at noon."

I saw his face change. For an instant he remained suspended in an anguished silence and then, like an ebb, a dark, fanatical expression came across his face.

"It doesn't matter," he said. "We have the night. We can start now and work through dawn."

"Tonight?" The idea appeared in front of me clear and terrible, as if taunting me. I looked at the clock. "Impossible," I said. "They're waiting for me for dinner."

"For *dinner?*" Roderer said, as though desperately searching for some other meaning in the word or to penetrate a hidden meaning. I got up calmly.

"For dinner, yes: people who eat around a table and say things like 'pass the salt' or 'this chicken is delicious.' "

I left without looking at him; I knew, above all, I shouldn't look at him. In two jumps, I was down the stairs and I walked home with long strides. I heard a rhythmic and malicious joy galloping inside me: *Pass the salt. This chicken is delicious.*

"Here you are, finally," my mother said. "What took you so long? Luckily, Anibal hasn't arrived yet."

"I went to the Olympus Club," I said, "and ran into Gustavo Roderer."

My sister came out of the kitchen. She was holding the silverware.

"What did you say?" she asked. When I repeated I had been with Roderer, she screamed.

"He couldn't get up!" she wailed and ran out desperately, throwing the silverware on the table. My mother and I stood there silently for an instant. I watched her go to the table and slowly set out the silverware.

"He's very sick," she said suddenly.

"I . . . didn't think it was anything serious."

"It's a very rare disease. Lupus. It's almost always fatal. But he wouldn't let them take him to the hospital."

"And Cristina's taking care of him?"

My mother nodded and went into the kitchen. I went to the bathroom to shower, hoping the gush of water would stun me, hoping that, for one minute, I could stop thinking. As I was about to get out, I heard a gentle knocking on the ground glass door. I opened it partially. It was my mother again.

"Anibal's here," she said. "He's in the living room. And your sister's still not back. I told him you'd gone out together. *Please,*" she begged. "Help me cover for her."

I said no, but when I saw her crushed expression, I finished dressing and went out the back door. Roderer's house was more than ten blocks away, almost in the far west edge of the town. The new mercury lamps of the hill hadn't gone that far out. There was just one street lamp on every road. They creaked as they swung in the wind and threw out shifting, yellowish circles into the center. Next to one of the wires I saw a herd of dogs devouring the ripped open scraps of a trash bag. They were still far away, but I slowed down. They saw me, too, and slowly shifted to occupy the street. I heard the noise pent up in their throats. *Dogs, the same as always,* I thought, but as

I passed between them, tense and hesitant, I couldn't bring myself to look at them.

It was hard to make out Roderer's house in the darkness. The garden in the entrance with the gravel path that his mother had cared for so well had disappeared and the climbing plants were invading the porch. Suddenly I heard a broken scream, the scream of someone suffering an inhuman agony. I stood still, listening, terrified in the silence. I waited for another sound, a wail, some sign that life was going on. Then I saw that the door was opening. An undecipherable figure stepped out and stopped under the arches of the porch, searching for something in his pockets. There was a crackle and I distinguished the face of Dr. Rago, barely lit by the street lamp. He was lighting his pipe. I approached him, anxiously. He didn't seem surprised to see me.

"How is Gustavo?"

"I think he's going to be better, now," he said. "Do you remember hepatic lupus? No? I often lectured about it, the classic example of ambulatory pain. *Supplicium Extremum:* the devouring of oneself. The antibodies stop recognizing the organs themselves and simply phagocytize them. The resulting pain is like no other. I have always found the sick in this condition, pacing from wall to wall, and voiceless from screaming. The only thing capable of calming them is morphine. When your sister came to find me it was the first thing I packed in my bag. But in this case," he stopped and took a drag, "there was a complication. The boy had, let me put it this way, a very high tolerance for morphine and at the same time a destroyed liver. The dose necessary to put him to sleep would have killed him. On the other hand, if I didn't inject him, he could survive only two or three hours until he went into cardiac arrest from exhaustion. Two or three more hours, absolutely lucid hours. Do you understand?" Rago scrutinized me. "No, you still can't understand. There was a detail: The boy wanted to say something. While I was attending him, he grabbed me and opened his mouth to say something, but of course, he couldn't articulate it through the pain. But he was totally conscious and he was fighting. The way he was struggling was moving. He might have been able to say it."

"What did you do?"

"I talked to your sister about it." Rago brought the pipe to his mouth and for an instant, the ember of the tobacco illuminated his face with a reddish glow. I thought I saw him smile. "Of course, I was absolutely certain we would concur. It was the humane thing to do, after all. And now," he said picking up his bag, "you'll understand, I have to go."

I entered the house. There was a single light at the end of the hall. I made my way past the empty rooms, guided in the darkness by the vague memory of my other visits. I opened the door to the room. Roderer was stretched out faceup, breathing laboriously. His eyes were half-closed. As if making a final, unconscious effort, they refused to close. My sister knelt by his side. When she saw me she made no motion, no sign, but I noticed she tensed up. Everything about her seemed to reject my presence there, as if I should not be attending that last ritual in which she officiated.

I tried not to make any noise as I approached.

"Cris . . . ," I called her softly, "Cristina . . ."

My sister gestured for me to be quiet. Roderer seemed to be muttering something, as if he'd seen a final light and was fighting to emerge from an invincible sleepiness. We leaned over him. His eyes opened slowly, amazingly. He didn't look at me or my sister. He looked above us. His hands reached out palms up, and as if he were knocking on some remote, high door, he whispered with a voice already not of this world: "Let me in, I am the first."